# SPEAR OF DESTINY

## PAUL McDERMOTT

*Paul McDermott*
*October 2025*

Beaten Track
www.beatentrackpublishing.com

The Spear of Destiny

Second Edition
Published 2022 by Beaten Track Publishing
First edition published 2017
Copyright © 2017, 2022 Paul McDermott

All rights reserved.

No part of this publication may be reproduced, stored in a retrieval system, or transmitted, in any form or by any means, without the prior permission of the publisher, nor be otherwise circulated without the publisher's prior consent in any form of binding or cover other than that in which it is published and without a similar condition including this condition being imposed on the subsequent publisher.

The moral right of the author has been asserted.

Paperback ISBN: 978 1 78645 549 9
eBook ISBN: 978 1 78645 550 5

Cover Design: TBA

Beaten Track Publishing,
Burscough, Lancashire.
www.beatentrackpublishing.com

# THE SPEAR OF DESTINY

# Chapter One

OBERLEUTNANT Herbert Nollau stood with his Zeiss night glasses glued to his eyes, impervious to the rain whipped across his cheeks by half a gale. This howled almost exactly at ninety degrees to the tide, which had just reached the full but had not yet begun its retreat. His command craft, *U-534*, sat uneasily at anchor, dipping at bow and stern in the current, yawing appreciably as frequent force-ten gusts buffeted her broad flanks. Low, heavy rainclouds hunkered closer, seeming to settle on the upper branches of the natural pine forest, which spread untamed, unculled, across the low hills of Schleswig-Holstein.

An identical pair of black Opel staff cars bracketed a canvas-bodied Mercedes half-track transport wagon, all three vehicles picking their way carefully along an unmarked country road. The headlights were taped down to the size and shape of a feral cat's vertical slits, acknowledging the strict rules governing all traffic during the hours of darkness. The road to the harbour just outside Lübeck was neither tarmacked nor enhanced with any form of lighting. The drivers were obliged to steer cautiously around every twist, using the gears and brakes more frequently than the accelerator.

*Amateurs!* he thought to himself, as the three sets of headlights crawled slowly closer. He would never trust any of them to navigate a submarine, and particularly not in circumstances which screamed out for discretion and secrecy. He'd followed their progress through the blackened landscape now for almost half an hour and was frankly amazed that nobody else appeared to have noted the convoy's progress. Once again, he scanned carefully behind the third set of lights: as far as he could tell, the vehicles conveying his final items of equipment weren't being followed. Perhaps there *was* a God to thank, after all.

He blanked the thought as soon as it intruded on his consciousness, forcing himself back into State-approved Wehrmacht thinking, based on purely practical matters directly related to carrying out current instructions with maximum efficiency, without question. He pulled the collar of his oilskins closer around his throat in a futile attempt to prevent the rain from seeping through, soaking his uniform. Raising his night glasses once more, he cursed the weather, the Wehrmacht and the world in general, feeling more exposed and vulnerable with every minute that passed as he waited for the convoy of lights to crawl closer, carrying the equipment which he had been ordered to collect. It bothered him that he was expected to set sail immediately and await orders concerning his destination by radio once he had cleared the bay and entered Store Bælt. Technically, that section of the North Sea was neutral Danish waters, and if he were to remain on the surface for any length of time...

As the lights snaked around another pair of curves and began their final descent to the shoreline and the jetty where *U-534* was waiting, Herbert Nollau mused that he had on board a much more powerful sender/receiver than any other U-boat. In fact, not just one but *two* radios equipped with the Enigma cryptographic programme had been installed, ostensibly for testing. With a sudden jolt, the deceptively young-looking oberleutnant realised that this technology was far more sophisticated than that which had previously been regarded as the best in the world: apart from being guaranteed unbreakable as a code, it could also send and receive radio signals without his craft needing to surface.

He shook his head to clear the worst of the pools that had formed in the upturned brim of his sou'wester and made his way down the ladder bolted to the side of the conning tower, aiming to be waiting on the quay before the three vehicles wheezed to a halt. His mechanic's ear analysed and diagnosed a list of faults he could clearly identify from the laboured chugging of each engine. Furious at this indication of inefficiency, a corner of his mind decided he would have had the senior officer responsible for each vehicle court-martialled if the decision had been up to him. In spite of the horrors he had witnessed in three years of naval warfare, he shuddered. His orders, distasteful though they might be, were crystal clear.

Two gaunt, silent shadows slid with simultaneous choreography from the rear seat of each of the Opels. Their sleek, black trench coats almost touched the planks of the jetty, glistening in the starlight as if the officers wearing them had been marching for hours in the rain rather than just stepping out of a warm, dry car. Nollau fired off his most formal salute; the four SS officers responded with a world-weary, bent-elbow half salute and pointedly refrained from returning Nollau's "Heil, Hitler!" One detached himself for a moment and gave a hand signal to the driver of the canvas-sided truck. The driver immediately hammered his fist twice on the bulkhead behind his seat. Four soldiers appeared over the tailgate of the wagon and began to manoeuvre something long and heavy out of the cargo space.

Turning to face his command meant that Herbert Nollau had to turn his back on the four staff officers. Somehow he managed to do this with an insolence which stated quite clearly that, as far as he was concerned, they were barely worthy of his contempt.

He placed a small, shrill whistle to his lips and blew, one long but not overloud blast. Within ten seconds, the deck was populated by about twenty matelots, standing at ease, who contrived to arrive from nowhere and in total silence. Close to the bows, and just for'ard of 'midships, cables were deployed from two small jib cranes. Within seconds, the submariner crew were on the jetty, taking the unidentified cargo from the shoulders of the four soldiers and hoisting it with ease onto the foredeck, thence by some lightning-fast *legerdemain* out of sight below decks. The crew followed, leaving Oberleutnant Nollau as the only member of the Senior Service still on the jetty. At a silent gesture from one of the anonymous black trench coats, the four soldiers climbed back over the tailgate, into the truck. After about four attempts, the driver managed to coax the engine into life and began to back and fill until he was facing the way he had come.

As he completed the manoeuvre and gunned the engine to set off up the hill, the four SS officers opened their trench coats to reveal the muzzles of rapid-fire MP40 machine pistols. With one accord, they raised their weapons and sent round after deadly round of ammunition into both the cab and the rear of the vehicle, holding the triggers steady. Before the hail of bullets ceased, the fuel tanks of the wagon exploded, sending flames soaring high into the night sky, setting small fires in the treetops as they lost their intensity and curled back towards the ground.

Suddenly, Herbert Nollau's orders seemed fractionally less dishonourable.

Having discharged their weapons, the four executioners appeared to have rediscovered some of their habitual swagger and pride. Crashing the butts of the now-empty guns against the rough wooden planking of the jetty they raised their right arms to the fullest, and screamed, *"Heil, Hitler!"* as their heels crashed together in perfect unison.

Sick to his stomach at the pleasure his countrymen took from the callous murder of fellow Germans, it was all Herbert

Nollau could do to raise his arm, bent-elbowed, in the less formal salute he would never under normal circumstances have accepted from others nor used himself. His pulse began to hammer at twice, perhaps three times its normal speed as he wheeled on his right heel and marched to cast off first at the sternpost of *U-534*, then, moving to the bow, coiled the short ropes and stowed them automatically before moving towards the conning tower as the U-boat drifted away from the quay. Through the deck, he felt her powerful engines throb against the soles of his feet, still idling in neutral until he gave the order to go slow ahead.

Before he could do that, however, there was the small matter of his final orders, which had been delivered in a private one-on-one briefing from Admiral of the Fleet von Friedeburg earlier that evening.

"You are an honourable man, Herbert. Every report I have read of your conduct throughout your three years as a U-boat commander has made this very clear to me. But for reasons which you will, I am sure, understand when the time comes, I am delivering these, the last orders you will ever receive as a commander in the German Navy, personally and as man-to-man. There will be *no* written records, and if therefore you should choose to ignore or even go directly against my orders, nobody will have witnessed this conversation and nobody will be in a position to accuse you of...of anything.

"But please be aware, I am *not* going to ask you to betray your country. Our country, which I know you love as much as I have always done, is finished as a world power. I think we both know that."

Without waiting for Nollau to reply, von Friedeburg swept on.

"Nor am I going to ask you to betray your command or perform any other abhorrent act such as scuttling your ship, which I know you love as much as you love being German!

Your choices, on the other hand, are very limited. If you are still here at midnight—" he glanced at his watch "—an hour and a half from now, you will have to make an unpalatable decision. Either you must accept an order to surrender, which, at this moment, has *not* yet been given, or you must stand and fight with what *limited* weaponry you have—but I do not think you would last very long against the might of Europe, with the Allied Armies heading this way from every direction possible. I do not think you would consider it the 'honourable' thing to do, either."

Since the admiral had departed in a powerful launch, Nollau had dissected his instructions, word by word, looking for some leeway, some opportunity to follow the letter of the law without observing each and every horrific detail. What he had been told he must do had seemed both repulsive and dishonourable, but after witnessing the massacre of unsuspecting German lives, shot in the back without a chance to defend themselves, he now had a clear conscience. The senior commander of the German Navy had effectively told him that he would be able to choose how to act once he left this isolated wharf, but he had been *very* specific about the last thing Nollau was required to do *before* leaving.

Halfway from the bows to the conning tower, he dropped to one knee and took careful aim through the sights of a rocket launcher. At this range, it was impossible to miss. Twin muzzles released the *ba-bam!* of two shells, which blew apart the two staff cars parked immobile on the jetty along with their occupants, four officers and two drivers. His orders had been quite specific: "There must be no witnesses."

Herbert Nollau was certain he could smell roasting flesh and realised it was not a youthful memory of *wildschwein*, the culinary masterpiece of his native Bavaria.

# Chapter Two

"Du, Søren!"
"Hvad?"

Jesper Bonde pointed almost due south over the stern of the battered jolle as they headed home to Gedser with the modest haul of shrimp and assorted small fish the two friends had managed to catch during the night. Søren squinted off into the distance, using his left arm to shield his eyes from the low, newly risen sun. Its rays danced across the wave tips, making it difficult to ascertain fine details, but there was something, a shadow, perhaps?

"Dammit, Jesper! What is it? D'you reckon it's a shoal? Maybe we should have stayed on station a bit longer."

He looked ruefully at their catch, barely enough to justify them chancing the wrath of the German Occupying Forces by breaking the night's curfew in an attempt to feed their families.

Jesper shook his head.

"That's no shoal of fish, and in these waters, it's not a whale either. I'll tell you this much, though. It's something bigger than any ordinary fish! It can only be a submarine, so the only question that matters is—friend or foe?"

The two fishermen's minds worked on similar lines, and both were immediately grateful that Jesper's jolle had a non-metallic hull and was sail-powered: they were unlikely to show up as a *blip!* on anyone's radar screen.

The telltale wake passed them at a safe distance—at least half a nautical mile, Jesper thought—and continued to spread behind the craft's bulk as it headed a few points north of west. As they watched, the first ripple from the unseen vessel's passage thumped under their keel; the light craft reacted by bobbing just hard enough for the difference to be noticeable. As Jesper continued to watch, the telltale wake began to veer very slightly right, and he continued to watch until he was certain of the change of course.

"Store Bælt, Søren. He's set a course east of Fyn, through Store Bælt!"

For his part, Søren Rappe was still gazing south, over the tiller. There was a speculative frown across his features.

"He's altered course, you say? Heading north on Store Bælt?"

"Far as I can make out."

"Look at this, will you?"

There was a definite nuance to Søren's voice that screamed of his inner suspicions. Jesper bit his tongue and gave the straits which separated Lolland from Germany his full attention. Suddenly he realised what had caught his companion's eye.

"We're still rocking from his wake! That shouldn't be possible!"

"It's possible, Jesper, but he'd have to be pretty deep and travelling flat out to cause *that* much wake from any depth. And let's face it. It's not *that* deep anywhere around here— fifty metres at most, I'd say."

"Where are they going? What are they doing?"

"I couldn't even begin to guess! But I believe it's time to find someone who can make more of this information than we can."

Jesper looked at Søren soberly, then cupped his hands around his mouth and chirruped like a small bird. It was the readily identifiable trill of a canary, which doubled as the call sign of the Danish Resistance. With no further discussion, they piled on every stitch of sail and added their personal efforts with two sets of oars until the jolle was fairly flying home to the security of Gedser harbour.

\*\*\*

Running on electric motors, skimming as close as the lead helmsman dared to the seabed itself, two sleek shapes nosed along in close order. The lead U-boat, *U-3523*, was in effect acting as the eyes for both craft as they sneaked along with an all but inaudible hum from their electric motors at a depth of about sixty metres.

"We are approaching some wrecks, Hr. Kapitän."
"Try to maintain depth. Go round, not over."
"Aye, Kapitän. Right hand down, ten degrees east."
"Ten degrees east, aye."

The responses from *U-534* confirmed its immediate reaction to *U-3523*'s course changes. This was the one chance which had to be taken. Total radio silence would have been preferable but impossible to achieve in the relatively shallow, well-trafficked waters that separated the main islands of Denmark. Although the country had only been on the periphery of combat, five years of warfare had left their mark, and the seabed had more than its fair share of unmarked, unrecorded shipwrecks and ditched aircraft that didn't appear on any submarine charts, and minimal radio contact between the two submarines was therefore unavoidable.

As the sea wolves inched their way north, the lead vessel drifted close to an amorphous shape, which had probably been a surface vessel in its previous incarnation. The voracious appetites of lichen, barnacles and other assorted flora and fauna native to these waters had been swift and greedy in attaching themselves to any surface which promised some form of sustenance or protection from the elements, and the outline of the vessel had become blurred beyond easy identification.

Herbert Nollau had the con of *U-534* himself. As the best navigator on board, he had taken the vessel out of harbour, and during the first hour he had allowed himself the pleasure of running the engines up to full power to check their reliability, should he need to call upon them for a sustained period of flight. Before the midnight hour mentioned in his verbal instructions, Nollau had achieved a successful rendezvous with *U-3523*. His orders had been very specific. The escort U-boat was intended solely for the protection of *U-534*, her crew and her cargo.

"Ultimately, both your escort vessels are to be considered expendable," the admiral had informed him. He might as well have been discussing the humane killing of an injured stray dog for all the emotion he showed.

"And are there no...written orders for this mission?"

"No, Oberleutnant Nollau. The main reason for that is the extremely fluid nature of the war effort at the moment, and also the extremely high level of security involved. Information and instructions are delivered in personal meetings whenever possible and on a need-to-know basis. I have no need to know where you will be heading, and that is why you will receive your final orders once you are underway.

"You can rest assured you will be informed in good time once you have met your escort. You must also be able to confirm that you are heading north and are not being followed. There will be certain pieces of equipment on board which will make such high-security communication possible. That is one reason for the lack of written orders. You can also regard the orders you receive underway as a final test for the equipment you are to carry to a secure location, one which has been selected as the fallback position from which the war will be conducted and won!"

This level of panic, and the flimsy excuse of 'national security', was beyond what even a young and relatively inexperienced oberleutnant could be expected to believe. Herbert Nollau was cynical enough to understand that he was likely to be left increasingly to his own devices with every desperate day that passed.

"I am perhaps overstepping my authority," the black trenchcoated murmured, "but I can confirm that the standing orders awaiting you at your rendezvous will be addressed to *Kapitän* Nollau, along with travel documents and further details of the newly commissioned Destroyer class vessel waiting for you."

Nollau caught himself replaying this scene from his rapidly dwindling stock of pleasant memories.

He tightened his grip on the controls fractionally, compensating for the fact that he'd allowed himself to drift dangerously close to an overarching structure, possibly the remains of a sturdy ship which had come to rest on the seabed almost upside down. In a first-aid manual, it would have been described as the three-quarter-prone position recommended for drowning victims; somehow, the comparison seemed to Nollau particularly appropriate.

"Rudder, half left. Decrease power port side by two knots, twenty seconds."

*There!* Situation dealt with, and not a tremor of self-doubt in the voice! The promised promotion was indeed long overdue, in *his* opinion.

His sternpost eased away from the wreck, as he had envisaged, but then began to droop towards the seabed as the vessel lost way due to the reduced speed. That had *not* been part of his calculations! Suddenly, he realised that the twenty-second period he had asked his engine room to observe would risk dragging his tail section along the seabed, alerting any asdic/radar operative in the area to the as-yet-undiscovered presence of *U-534*, followed, inevitably, by a shower of depth charges.

For an eternal split second, he reconsidered his decision to cut power to his port engine and concluded that the possibility of audible engine noise was preferable to the noise of his tail dragging the bottom and damaging the hull. The decision, however, was taken out of his hands a moment later when the signal from the lead sub came early and did not follow the agreed pattern.

The chime was replaced by a staccato burst of klaxon horn, interspersed with the *ping!* that indicated depth charges tumbling towards them.

As he took the con once more and toggled for full control of the twin engines, he was aware of a throb of powerful diesels as the lead submarine crammed on every available ounce of power and made her attempt to lead their unseen surface adversary away from *U-534* and her tail gunner. Two dull *thwomps* indicated that the first pair of depth charges had detonated somewhere ahead of them and at a depth shallow enough not to cause *U-534* any structural damage. When the concussion wave arrived a few seconds later, Nollau was ready for it and replied with a complicated manipulation of his controls which allowed him to 'ride' the underwater wave by showing the smallest possible surface area—the nose of the craft—to the direction of the charges so that the underwater wave passed *beneath* the sub. He found he was holding his breath. This was an exercise which he had only ever been informed about in *theory*.

The invisible wave stirred the mud and sand of the seabed, pillowing the sternpost just before it made contact with the rocks and the scattered detritus from the overhanging wreck. Simultaneously, the port engine kicked in and caught the weight of the vessel as neatly as an alert slip fielder at Lords, giving Nollau full control of the vessel and making him master once more of his own destiny.

He paused with his hands relaxed on the controls, forced himself to read through the variety of screens on his console showing the relative depths and positions of the two U-boats, any rocks in the vicinity and other fixed obstacles such as wrecks. Most importantly, it showed the approximate position of surface craft close enough to register on the screens.

As he watched, *U-3523* shot forward and began to make off in a nor-nor-westerly direction, challenging the hunter on the surface to give chase. Now, the most important question was, did the captain of the surface vessel know there were two U-boats beneath his keel, or would he fall for the feint?

*Run or wait?* Nollau had to decide. It had to be the *right* decision. He wouldn't get a second chance.

He studied the screens around his con post one more time, reading them like a three-dimensional chessboard. His hands rested lightly on the controls. The engine purred in neutral, and the sensitive depth gauge informed him that his tail no longer drooped. *U-534* had regained a perfectly balanced horizontal plane and was able to move off in almost any direction, if evasive action were deemed necessary.

The lightest of simultaneous feather touches on for'ard and stern starboard controls was enough to give him the one positional shift which could not have been expected or predicted by the commander of any surface craft watching for an indication of movement. *U-534* responded by drifting lazily, inch by perfectly balanced inch, concealing her presence *under* the overhang of the wreck.

All he had to do now was hold his nerve, play possum for a few short minutes, watch his screens for some sort of confirmation that no enemy shipping remained on the surface to track him.

As he gazed intently at his screens, consciously willing every member of his disciplined crew to be fully aware of his immediate surroundings and to maintain a rigid, unbroken silence, he had a momentary vision which was so powerful he later used what was to become the final entry in his daily log to sketch his vision of a new, improved radar screen, which he described as a 3D cube.

Three agonising, treacle-slow minutes oozed by, according to the silently sweeping second hand of the ship's chronometer hung above the command hub and clearly visible from all sides. There were a number of stifled coughs and the suspicion of a sneeze, which almost had one unfortunate matelot passing out in his brave attempt to defuse it, but patience was rewarded when the faintest possible *ping!* on the asdic screen coincided almost to the second with an underwater ripple catching *U-534*'s bulk, causing her to bob fractionally as it passed.

The signal had originated from a position some distance to the north and east, relative to his position: Nollau realised the enemy vessel had opted to pursue *U-3523*, creating for him the opportunity he needed. Now it was possible to slip through the ambush at the narrow point close to the east coast of Fyn, just where the straits broadened to become the Kattegat—open waters where he could run and hide at will.

Cautiously, he eased his nose out from under the wreck he had utilised to disguise his presence and realised he had, without thinking about it, ignored the random phantom readings it had produced, which now disappeared. The main screens remained clear: the sea wolf had managed to avoid the surface hunting pack, though possibly at the cost of his protective screen. Now it was imperative for him to complete his mission, if only to atone for the unquestioning self-sacrifice of the escort vessel and its crew.

# Chapter Three

Long shadows sprawled on the cobbled main street of Gedser as Jesper and Søren made their way from the jetty to the nearest *værtshus*. Each carried two full buckets of fresh fish, some of which they would barter for a decent breakfast and a couple of beers. Barter was the preferred business method nowadays, particularly since the German Occupying Forces had attempted to introduce their worthless scraps of coloured paper as an alternative to the Danish krone. Mute insolence on the Danish side combined with a lack of decision in Germany had resulted in the proposition being quietly dropped.

Despite the early hour, Jesper and Søren were not the only ones in town both awake and about their business. The proprietor of the village kro, Ib Andersen, had been up before dawn, brewed an urn of coffee and baked fresh morning bread. He had just laid two places at Jesper's favourite table when they walked in.

"Any chance of a breakfast for two cold, hungry fishermen?" called Søren, stepping nimbly out of his rubber boots, leaving them next to Jesper's at the door to keep the waxed wooden floor clean. A cheerful blaze poked through the log fire, awakening tiny flickering spirits to dance in the horse brasses that covered the walls.

Ib dried his hands carefully on a towel, which he folded neatly and tucked back into his waistband. He inspected the proffered buckets of fish, selected two fair-sized cod and filled a pint glass with shrimp before heading for the kitchen. By the time Jesper and Søren had settled themselves, he was back with a full pot of coffee, two shot glasses and a bottle of aquavit wrapped in a pristine clean cloth to protect the fingers of the pourer from rime frost.

"Will you join us, Ib?"

These were the first words spoken aloud since the greeting made on entry, but the silence which had prevailed until that moment was one of camaraderie and mutual respect, being neither secretive nor uncomfortable. Ib murmured his thanks and swiftly laid an extra place for himself.

"How was the fishing?"

Søren looked up from pouring a round of schnapps and indicated Jesper should consider himself the spokesman.

"Yeah, well, you saw what we brought with us. You got the opportunity to choose whatever you fancied!"

"Østresøen doesn't have anywhere near the fish in it we used to catch…before…"

Even after almost three years, Ib still found it difficult to admit out loud that his beloved country had been invaded by their traditional enemies from the south.

Jesper and Søren nodded their agreement and raised their shot glasses in silent toast to the Dannebrog, the symbol of national pride draped defiantly above the pub's central chimney breast. Every so often, there was a half-hearted German effort to outlaw this practice, but to date, none had been effective.

"*Jamen du*, Ib. We need to make contact with your friend from Slagelse," Jesper said, lining up the three now-empty schnapps glasses on the chessboard-inlaid tabletop. He placed them on three adjoining black squares, running diagonally away from his corner of the table.

"Not easy," murmured Ib. "The Germans have made radio contact a risky business recently. They raided a farm in Sørø, not far from Slagelse, and executed the whole family when they found an old, useless valve radio in one of their barns."

"Morons! Couldn't they see it was a commercial radio only capable of receiving studio broadcasts?"

"Morons is about right, Jesper. Apparently, they killed all the livestock they could find and burnt the carcasses in one great heap!"

"What a total waste, Ib! All they had to do, was—"

"Take over the running of the farm themselves or hire another family to run it? There was no need to kill all the livestock. No way could that amount of meat be sold or stored before it spoilt!"

"All the same, Ib, it's vital we get a message to the Canary."

"It won't be easy. Everyone's on edge, and the Germans have stepped up their damned stop-and-search exercises. It's getting to be a planned operation to cross the bridge to Falster!"

Lolland was the largest of a tight group of three islands, but all traffic with the mainland was routed through Falster. Møn, a much smaller island, completed the trio: many of the houses on it were holiday homes of rich and influential Danes but had been commandeered by the Occupying Forces as soon as it was discovered that the houses were, for the most part, unoccupied and undefended.

"There's one way I think it can be done without arousing too much attention," Ib said as he split a hot bread roll in his hands. He layered a criminal amount of homemade butter onto it and watched it melt. "We're still able to play soccer matches. I can put together a team to play Slagelse, drive the coach myself. The Germans encourage us to keep up our sporting events—I'm sure they think it keeps us from fighting in the streets. I'll tell 'em it's a cup match. As long as we've enough diesel to fill the coach, they won't care!"

Jesper emptied the last of the coffee, sharing it as equally as he could between the three cups. Ib puckered a speculative eye into the schnapps bottle, from which the rime frost had now melted. There was enough in the bottom of the bottle to drip a taste into each coffee. With a wicked gleam in his eye, he raised his cup, and in a most unmusical voice, he sang a couple of lines of a well-known tune. It was the most unlikely combination for an unorthodox toast:

> "Scatter his enemies,
> And make them fall!"

Jesper and Søren stared at him as if he'd grown an extra head.

"Ib, you'll get us all locked up if anyone hears you!"

Despite the mangling caused by the singer's inability to hold a tune, combined with his lack of practice with the English language, the melody was recognisable as a couple of bars of the British National Anthem, something which would certainly have been punished if a patrol had chanced to push the door open and catch the barkeep *in flagrante delicto*.

Ib grinned and appeared to lose at least twenty-five years' worth of age wrinkles from his face. "Most English people couldn't sing the words to the second verse of the song. I doubt your typical sausage eater could, either!"

He continued to hum the tune, and when he had reached the end, he added the words:

> "O Lord, our God, arise,
> Scatter his enemies,
> And make them fall.
> Confound their politics,
> Frustrate their knavish tricks,
> On thee our hopes we fix:
> God save the King."

\* \* \*

Whether it was a feature of some deeply-ingrained racial memory or telepathy (or possibly even osmosis), the regular players of Gedser FC all found one reason or another to visit the village *kro* before the morning was half over. By midday, Ib had enough names to write up an official-looking team sheet and present it to Kommandant Brecht, who was nominally in charge of the GOP platoon responsible for security on Lolland, Falster and Møn.

"Slag...Slaw...however you say the name of this town?"

"Slagelse."

Ib gave exactly the information he had been asked for, nothing more.

"It appears to be on the main rail route across country, from Copenhagen to Esbjerg?"

"That is correct."

Kommandant Brecht looked Ib squarely in the eyes. "Hr. Andersen, I am aware of the...tension which exists between local residents and my troops. I do not approve of this animosity, and it will make my job here much easier if I could persuade you to convey my sympathies to your friends and neighbours? I didn't ask for this position, and from what I have seen, I do not expect to be here for very long, but that's a different matter entirely."

He seemed to realise that he was in danger of speaking out of turn and sought to change the subject.

"If I can have your assurance that there will be no amateur dramatics, such as an attempt to take an unauthorised trip to Copenhagen or the West Coast, and that everyone will return together on the bus, then I am prepared to allow this match to take place."

"There is one small matter..." Ib began and paused. This was the tricky bit.

"I don't think we can get back before nightfall. There is a tradition that we share a few beers with our opponents before leaving, and especially when we play Slagelse.

They have been our chief league rivals for many years! We need a pass of some sort in case we cannot get back home before the hour of curfew."

He stopped and waited, seemingly calm, but inside he was a jangle of nerves. Had his bluff worked?

Kommandant Brecht sat behind his desk and reached for a pen.

"Do you realise how much trouble this could cause me, personally, if you choose to abuse the trust I am placing in you?"

"I can assure you, Kommandant, I will give you my personal guar—"

"Be careful, Hr. Andersen! Don't make any promises you might regret! As it stands, I believe you to be an honourable man. I trust you to do whatever is necessary to make this football match a success and bring everyone home safely. I assume you have sufficient fuel for the trip? That is one thing I cannot help you with, I'm afraid."

"I've already checked, sir. That won't be a problem, although I shall try to persuade our friends in Slagelse to let us have anything they can spare before we start the return journey."

Fuel deliveries, especially for non-military purposes, had been at best sporadic for some time now in their region.

"How soon will you be leaving?"

"Most of the team have dropped in at my *værtshus* already this morning. We take our football seriously, you know, and especially against Slagelse! As long as all the kit has been collected, we can leave within the hour—and even that's going to mean it will be at least six o'clock before we finish the game. That's why the curfew permit is so important."

"*Aber, naturlich*, Hr. Andersen! I wish you and the team all the best of luck!"

\* \* \*

"Pastor Berning? I didn't know you were a member of the football squad?"

Ib stiffened as he heard the tiny twinge of doubt in Kommandant Brecht's voice. He caught himself holding his breath and forced himself to relax. He needn't have worried. The town's Catholic priest was more than ready for the question.

"The team won't get very far without a goalkeeper, Hr. Kommandant, and the Lord appears to have given me a safe pair of hands! Remember, the present Holy Father is a keen horseman, you know, and a brilliant violinist! There is nothing which prevents a priest from having a modest talent for skills other than those of the Church!

"Also, Catholics in Slagelse haven't had a priest of their own for the last three years or more, and I can say a Mass for them while we are there. An extra blessing for our noble footballers wouldn't do any harm, either!"

With a little banter and chaff, the team, their playing strip and a supply of rye bread topped with either cheese or salami for the journey were quickly assembled, and the coach departed in an impressive cloud of diesel fumes with Ib Andersen at the wheel.

On an empty country road, with excellent all-round visibility and no possibility of being surprised by meeting another vehicle, Fr. Berning tapped Ib on the shoulder.

"Pull into the next layby. I'll say Grace, and we can eat lunch."

'Layby' was something of a flattering description for the slight widening in the road which Ib pulled into, but there was room for at least two vehicles to pass on the road itself—or so Fr. Berning judged as Ib applied the handbrake and killed the engine. Grace was said, and Ib went around to open the bonnet to check the oil and water. As he climbed the steps, Fr. Berning asked him to turn on the engine.

Ib was surprised at this slightly odd request but turned the ignition key. The engine caught smoothly at the first time of asking. Fr. Berning was already halfway down the steps and on his way around to the front of the coach, carrying his perpetual black valise. It seemed rather heavy, certainly heavier than a bag containing a breviary, a few hosts and other small items a priest might need to serve his flock. Ib followed, thinking he might be needed to assist with whatever it was Fr. Berning had planned.

Before Ib arrived, the wiry priest had already emptied the standard paraphernalia—breviary, hosts, chalice, stole, biretta—from his bag and was removing a smooth plate, which proved to be a false base. He looked up as Ib approached.

"Here, I don't want to be stopped for longer than necessary. You can help by clamping these clips to the battery terminals!"

Without waiting to see if his orders were being carried out, Fr. Berning continued to assemble the components of a short-wave transceiver radio with all the speed and dexterity of one who has performed the same task times without number. Before Ib had clamped the terminals, the priest had finished assembling the radio and turned it on as soon as Ib gave him the nod. There was a slight hum as the valves warmed up, ready to transmit.

Fr. Berning's hand dipped once more into his bag: this time, a pair of Zeiss glasses appeared. In dumb show, Ib was asked to 'keep an eye on the road'.

"Lima Fox Five calling Sierra Golf. Come in."

After two repetitions, the answer came back: "Sierra Golf to Lima Fox Five. Receiving five by five."

"Thank you, Slagelse. This for your information: we will use our red-and-white striped shirts, except for the goalkeeper, whose shirt will be yellow."

"Message understood, Lima Fox Five, what is your ETA?"

"Perhaps thirty minutes—fourteen hundred, latest. We can hope for a kickoff at fifteen hundred."

"Understood, Lima Fox Five. Over and Out."

The radio was dismantled and vanished as quickly as it had appeared. Scanning the horizon, Ib was certain that nobody had been close enough to observe that the bus had been stationary for almost five minutes. Fr. Berning caught his eye and grinned.

"By and large, your average German falls into one of two categories. He's either highly superstitious and terrified of anything he can't pull apart to find out how it works then put it back together again—I'm told the Führer himself belongs to this side—or he's so utterly and completely rightwing Church that he's terrified of the thought of upsetting even the least important little village priest.

"Whichever he is makes no difference, as you can almost be certain that none of 'em would ever dream of challenging the cloth—or asking a priest what he's got at the bottom of his bag! Onward! Slagelse, here we come!"

\* \* \*

"Tell me it's none of my business, Father, and I'll shut up, but I guess the message about the colour of your jersey wasn't really...?"

Ib left the question hanging in the air as they approached the outskirts of Slagelse. It seemed as if it were only a few minutes after they had resumed their journey.

Fr. Berning crouched a little closer to Ib's ear and dropped his voice.

"That's correct, my friend, and since you're smart enough to have worked that out, I don't need to tell you that I'm trusting you—literally—with my life! If Kommandant Brecht or any of his superior officers ever found out...

"Anyway" he continued, calmly and soberly, "the Canary will make contact probably with someone who isn't playing, almost certainly while everyone's attention is focused on the match itself. He could even approach you, Ib, though as you haven't been with the team to Slagelse before today, the chances of that aren't high. The problem is, both Jesper and Søren are likely to be on the pitch, and they're both good players. We can't really manage without them."

"Can we rotate players during the game, do you think? Let someone play the first half of the match, perhaps, and then swop with another player?"

"Not sure the rules allow for that, or if Slagelse would be willing to try it out as an experiment, but I don't suppose there's any harm in asking our own players."

The level of security demonstrated as the coach carrying Gedser FC to their match came to the outskirts of Slagelse was typical of the low-key understandings which the Occupying Forces had initiated throughout the major towns and cities of Denmark and consisted of a 4x3 metre Icelandic tent daubed in camouflage colouring, with a folding table and two chairs in front of it. Two privates, armed with rifles that appeared older than the boy soldiers who carried them, stood at ease in the centre of the road, rifles at port on their left shoulders. Ib pulled to a halt and offered their travel documents for inspection.

The soldier who looked as if he might be slightly the elder of the two accepted the envelope and glanced at the name and address details.

"Moment, *bitte*!"

He turned and marched, envelope tucked under his free arm, to the nearest house. The German swastika fluttered from the flagpole in the centre of the front garden, indicating that the house had been requisitioned (or 'liberated') as HQ and offices for the commanding officer and his staff. He disappeared indoors for a few seconds, reappearing almost immediately with an officer in full dress uniform.

"Velkommen til!"

The officer's open, sincere smile was very welcome, and the fact that the CO had opted to use a Danish greeting phrase reinforced this. He offered a crisp salute as he paused at the open coach door, then glanced down at the letter he had been given.

"Team captain...Rappe?"

Søren identified himself: he was sitting close to the door and moved forward to act as spokesman for the team.

The officer was even younger than he had at first appeared. Tipping his cap slightly with one forefinger, he addressed Søren with a friendly, slightly formal tone to his voice:

"I'm sorry, but saying 'Hello!' is about as far as I've got with learning Danish yet! Still, there are similarities to German. It shouldn't take me..."

He appeared anxious to make a good impression, and Jesper also warmed to him immediately.

"However little you've learnt, Sir, you've made an effort—which is more than I can say about many of your countrymen in our part of the Kingdom of Denmark!"

The CO looked at the papers again and nodded enthusiastically. "I see you are here to play a football game."

"Match" Jesper muttered and immediately flushed at his own impertinence. How dare he interrupt a senior officer of the barely tolerated German Occupying Forces?

A split second later, when he realised that he had been addressed in English and automatically corrected the speaker in the same language, he felt just a little apprehensive. Was his knowledge of the enemy's language going to count against him?

The CO inspected Jesper closely with a curious look in his eyes. Jesper couldn't decide if it was one of suspicion or...amusement?

After a second or two, the CO smiled, and the tension melted away.

"My father and mother were both language teachers, and they encouraged me to learn at every...chance. My English is better zan my Danish."

Jesper noted that the CO had the usual problem pronouncing the soft 'th' sound.

"But I think you might outscore me?"

"Herr Kommandant—"

"Kapitän, bitte!"

"My apologies, Captain! I'm not familiar with German badges of rank as yet."

"Accepted, Mr....?"

"Bonde, Captain. Jesper Bonde. And my English is as good as any Dane's. We are required to pass exams in English and German before we leave school."

"I see! So, when you corrected me by saying 'match' instead of 'game'...?"

"Talking about a match between equals is much more likely than referring to it as a game for someone who has lived any time in England, as opposed to someone who learnt his English in a classroom," Jesper explained with a smile intended to smooth ruffled feathers. It seemed to work: the CO offered his hand in greeting.

"I will detail a motorcyclist to guide you to the clubhouse if you wish?"

"That won't be necessary. We've played at this club at least twice every season, since...since before I was born, I think!" A chorus of chuckles and good-humoured laughter masked the odd muttered curse of all things German which some of the more nationalistic elements of the team might have thought to utter.

The two armed sentries gave way, and Ib was allowed to drive the coach through the checkpoint and onto the sports ground. By the same inexplicable combination of telepathy and osmosis, word of their coming had rippled ahead of them, and there were already two or three members of the

Slagelse team waiting to greet them when they trundled up to the gates.

"I see the jungle drums are still working well," grunted Søren as he negotiated the holdall containing the team shirts down the steps and off the bus.

"We've not been idle since we got word." There was no chance of them being overheard, but the speaker dropped his voice as he ended the sentence and glanced around.

Father Berning bustled forward, carrying his scuffed black valise.

"It's best if I leave this in the vestry. That way, I can go straight to the church as soon as I've showered after the match. Can you get word to the congregation that I should be able to say Mass at…let's say, five o'clock?"

It lacked a few minutes for two o'clock, but the pitch was already being marked with lime and the two goals were in position. More of the home team arrived, and the first spectators began to drift in, a mixture of older men whose playing days were well past, and a number of pre-teen future stars. The latter had a ball with them and immediately began kicking it about but had the sense not to encroach on the marked-up pitch. Most of the older men had brought refreshments with them: some had cloth bags under their arms, others small wooden crates to sit upon in lieu of the non-existent seating benches. Bags and crates alike soon proved to contain bottles of the local pilsner.

Within minutes, or so it seemed, the entire population of Slagelse had arrived to watch the match. The beer began to talk as the fans rooted for their favourites and insulted their visiting rivals, but it was all good-humoured. Jesper led his team onto the pitch. Father Berning, looking ten years younger in his goalkeeping jersey, trotted behind him as they made their way to the centre circle. When they arrived, the team formed an approximate semicircle, facing the priest. In one smooth, choreographed movement, they all dropped to one knee as Fr. Berning raised his hands and blessed the team, something he had done before every match since he had become a regular team member, mainly because it seemed to disconcert their opponents. Slagelse, of course, had seen this demonstration before and realised that they were being challenged but somehow didn't quite dare risk the wrath of heaven with ribald comments or other forms of retaliation.

Fr. Berning trotted to one end of the pitch with a towel, a cap with a wide brim and a pair of leather gloves rolled in a neat bundle. As he kicked scuff marks to indicate the centre of the goalmouth and points on his six-yard line immediately in front of each post, a player wearing a Slagelse tracksuit and carrying a sports bag strolled up and waited to catch the keeper's eye.

*Hope he doesn't think he can intimidate me*, thought the priest. When he took off his collar, he had a habit of turning into a master tactician, an aggressive win-at-all-costs player.

The player said nothing but placed his holdall between his feet and waited for Fr. Berning to complete his preparations. As he turned to walk back to stand in the centre of the goalmouth, he noticed that although the holdall was almost zipped shut, a few inches of a towel or similar item had escaped. It was yellow in colour…their eyes met. Fr. Berning deliberately flicked his gaze from the player's face, down to the holdall and back: twice, so there could be no mistake.

Strolling to his bundle, Fr. Berning shook out his gloves, then rolled his cap inside his yellow towel. The sun was still high enough in the sky, he wouldn't need the cap before the second half, maybe not at all.

His defenders trotted towards him, dribbling a spare ball between them. He trotted out to join them at the edge of the penalty area, so as not to cut up and muddy the goalmouth while they loosened up for a few minutes prior to kickoff. When he turned to go back and take up his start position, the Slagelse player had drifted away. Glancing to the corner where he had left his equipment, he noticed that his towel was now tucked inside the capacious headgear. He decided that, for the moment, the safest thing was to ignore this tiny detail and act as if he hadn't noticed it at all. A number of pale-grey German uniforms had begun to drift through the club's single entrance gate. He had to assume that, with no prospect of any alternative entertainment, a substantial majority of those not working would turn up to cheer on one team or the other: there was no reason the German Occupying Forces would stay away.

By the time the game kicked off, there were a surprising number of spectators sitting, standing or crouching four and five deep on both sides of the pitch, and a sprinkling of others—younger children and teenagers who would have had difficulty seeing over the adults along the touchlines— had spread out along the other two sides of the pitch from corner flag to goalmouth. Whenever the ball left the pitch, it was returned within seconds for the throw-in, goal kick or corner necessary to continue the game. The pace of the game was fast and furious, but scrupulously fair. Several chances were created at both ends, but when the referee's whistle brought the first half to an end, neither side had managed to score.

A bucket full of halved oranges for each team was carried out by a junior club member: Jesper glanced around and decided it wasn't worth going all the way back to the changing rooms for the half-time break. He nodded towards the far end of the pitch, the end they would defend during the second half.

"We can just as easily squat in the 'D' and talk tactics. We've done well this first half, but I don't fancy extra time or a penalty shootout. We have to up our game, poke in a winner during the second half!"

Fr. Berning moved into the centre of the circle where he couldn't be seen from the touchlines. Opening out his towel, he sketched a casual cross in the air, provoking a Pavlovian reaction from the rest of the team, who crossed themselves.

Fr. Berning looked up.

"Thanks for following the hint. The sausage eaters will think we're praying and leave us alone!" He opened out a single sheet of paper as he spoke.

"I've been contacted by the Canary—either personally or via a go-between, but that's not important. What matters is, I left a report of what Jesper and Søren saw heading for Store Bælt—seems incredible so much has happened on one day, but it was only this morning."

"Any idea what speed a U-boat can make running deep?" a young voice asked.

Fr. Berning frowned. "Careful, Lars! Keep your voice down, even if we are out of range of casual listeners. Jesper and Søren might be able to hazard a guess, but it would probably take a naval expert to know for certain."

Søren looked at Jesper, who shook his head.

"Nah, didn't think you'd have any better idea than me! All I can say is, from the wake we saw, there had to be at least two of 'em, and they were moving pretty quickly, without even trying to hide."

"Perhaps they didn't expect to be observed at that time of day," offered Jesper.

Søren nodded. "That's probably close enough, Jesper," he said and turned to the pastor. "Is there anything we need to know in the document you've received?"

Fr. Berning glanced at it again. "There's nothing which leaps off the page at me. What there is I'll let you know when we get back to Gedser. Meanwhile, we've got a match to win!"

The second half of the match began in much the same manner as the first half had ended, with the visitors in constant attack, held at bay by some dogged resistance. Despite the rivalry that had developed over many years between the two teams, the match remained cleanly fought, with no reasons for the referee to interrupt the cut-and-thrust, end-to-end pulse of the game. As the non-stop action began to take its toll, the never-say-die tenacity of the visiting fishermen gave them the advantage over the host team, and a slightly fortunate very late goal from a forced corner proved decisive. There was barely time to jog back to the centre circle and restart the game before the final whistle blew and Gedser were through to the next round.

\*\*\*

"Get the kitbag, and those who aren't going to be at Mass, onto the bus and stay there. I want to leave ASAP without seeming rude."

"We can't leave without drinking a beer with them! That would be suspicious—and I doubt Slagelse would ever forgive us!"

"So have a crate ready at the side of the coach. All we have to do is flash the permit at them and say we've given our word to get back as close to curfew time as we can. That's not too far from the truth, anyway!"

As the majority of the travelling team were non-Catholics, this was easy to arrange and convincingly innocent of all possible subterfuge or attempt at deception. When Fr. Berning arrived back at the coach in the company of the three members of the team who were RC, both teams assembled in an approximate semicircle, ready to drink a 'standing glass'.

"You'll not get rid of us this easily next time, I promise!"

As team captain, it fell to Jesper to find an appropriate comment to cover the slight embarrassment both teams felt at the speedier-than-usual departure.

"Yeah, well, there's a shortage of beer at the moment, and our match winner's too young to enjoy one himself anyway."

Lars Bauer, who'd scored the late decider, grinned self-consciously and turned almost the same colour as his flame-red hair with embarrassment. A few ribald comments were flung in his direction, without malice.

"Still, we won't tell your dad if you take a sip. You deserve it. How does a shrimp like you climb that high to head in a corner?"

Lars was the sixteen-year-old son of the head of a successful music school in Nykøbing Falster, and a promising cellist in the school orchestra. He declined the offer and took an extra bottle of lemonade instead.

"All the same, we'll expect you to make a good job of it next time we visit you!" Jesper growled as they tidied everything away and boarded the bus.

The war, and the inevitable shortages which were caused by rationing, were *verboten* as far as topics of conversation were concerned. On the other hand, this was an oblique reference to their present circumstances, a sly dig, which the Occupying Forces would have difficulty understanding even if they were quick enough to follow the speed of delivery. Honour was satisfied and a promise made that the next match, whenever it might be played, would be 'special' and would be feted in suitable fashion. Bottles were swiftly emptied and ceremoniously returned to the empty crate: recycling was another unavoidable fact of life, especially in a country at war.

\* \* \*

Shadows were lengthening as the coach passed Næstved, roughly the halfway point on their journey. Fr. Berning stood, stretched, and asked Ib to pull into the next convenient layby.

"You all know why we came to play this outstanding fixture today, so I won't waste time going through the details. I'll just say this. The message was successfully passed on—we all know who it was for, even if none of us know his name or what he looks like.

"The local group are now on full alert and thank us for the warning. They will do their best to get a message back to us one way or another. Now, this is as good a chance as any to give thanks..."

His calm confidence carried hope and comfort for all denominations and those of none in particular: everyone bowed his head and listened in silence as the priest prayed briefly in the comforting warmth of the late-afternoon sun.

\*\*\*

"Young Lars had another good game today, Frank! He scored the winner, too, saved us playing extra time!"

Frank's bushy, snow-white eyebrows shot up, and his lived-in, weathered features crinkled with unfeigned pleasure at Ib's one-line assessment of the contribution his son had made to the important game against the 'old enemy' from Slagelse.

"I'm glad you weren't delayed getting back. He needs to practise a Mozart piece before the concert tomorrow afternoon."

Frank's mock severity was perfectly matched by Lars' insincere groan of reluctance at the prospect of having an extra hour of cello practice as his 'reward' for scoring the winning goal in a football match. Everybody knew that Lars lived for music, and the same applied to his father. He'd been a late but most welcome surprise to Frank, who had been approaching his half-century when Lars was born. Tragically, his mother had died of complications arising from Lars' birth, and Frank had raised him single-handed.

Frank's music school had grown from modest beginnings and was now starting to attract attention from further afield. This included several towns along the North German coast where a number of schools had made enquiries about sending their most promising pupils to him. Having had almost all his language tuition direct from native speakers,

Frank spoke fluent 'gutter Parisian' and 'urchin Cockney'. His Danish leant more towards Esbjerg than Copenhagen, but his Italian was unmistakably Roman. Frank's German origins were common knowledge locally, but the very idea of currying favour with the Gestapo by denouncing him was utterly unthinkable. Before long, the very fact that the Occupying Forces were unaware of the true origins of a prominent local personality became the cause of many a sly comment in *værtshuse* throughout the region.

Showered and changed, Lars headed for the kitchen where Frank had prepared a filling meal of meatballs, red cabbage and boiled potatoes.

"We're lucky this island has always been able to grow all the food Denmark needs," Frank said as they cleared the table and washed up. The island group had earned its nickname as the 'South Sea Islands' of Scandinavia, and agriculture had always been its most valuable resource. Even after almost six years of wartime deprivations, locally grown produce was still keeping everyone who lived in the region well fed.

Household chores complete, father and son strolled unhurriedly to the 'business end' of the converted farmhouse, where Frank had built an acoustically perfect concert room and half a dozen soundproofed practice rooms. Frank chose the nearest of the practice rooms and waited for Lars to enter: he stood at the door and made sure it was properly closed before following his son to the piano in the opposite corner. Lars went to sit by his cello, but Frank shook his head.

"Lars, you know as well as I do that you could play that piece in your sleep. I felt I had to say something to Ib—and the rest of the team—just in case there was someone listening who…might not be entirely trustworthy."

"Dad, surely you trust everyone on the team? You can't think—"

"Lars, I don't believe for a moment there's anyone on the team who isn't a true Dane! But there's always the chance that someone could be pressured to give up information, however insignificant it might seem, if they felt that they—or their family—might be at risk if they didn't cooperate with the Occupying Forces."

Despite his country of birth, Frank found it hard to use the terms 'German' or 'Germany' and had made a habit of finding other ways of referring to the country and its occupants. His original passport had been conveniently 'lost' soon after he had married Lars' mother, and he had pounced on his first opportunity to replace it with its Danish equivalent.

He sat opposite Lars now, with no attempt to pretend that they were there to rehearse for a concert.

"We're sitting here because the soundproofing makes this room absolutely secure. Nobody can eavesdrop."

He paused and made sure he has Lars' full attention.

"I know why this match was played today, and I know who Pastor Berning was hoping to meet. There's not much you can tell me I don't already know. I'm one of only half a dozen people who has actually spoken to the Canary over the last five years or so, though we've never met. Did Pastor Berning manage to meet…anyone?"

Lars nodded. "He told us at half-time that he'd been contacted while we were still warming up before the match even started. I don't know if the 'contact' stayed to watch the game, or if it was the Canary or someone sent by him."

"Sounds well organised. But there's something more important I need to tell you, Lars, and that's why I needed to make sure nobody else could be listening."

Lars stiffened. He'd had to grow up quickly, and his father had treated him as an equal, almost like a younger brother, since he'd reached his teenage years. He sensed that whatever was on his father's mind was something significant and of crucial importance.

"You know we've got five promising musicians with the school at the moment whose families live 'over the water'," he began.

Lars nodded. "Yes. Four violins and a clarinet."

Typically, Lars identified the students by instrument rather than name. Frank suspected his son might struggle to put names to the students, despite there being no more than thirty pupils enrolled in the school altogether.

"I need you to promise me now that you'll be very careful what you say if and when any of them are close by. In particular, I need you to think twice—and even three, four times—before you let slip that I...let's say, if I've gone to Copenhagen, perhaps at short notice or none at all. I'll make sure that there's someone to take care of lessons and tuition if I have to go somewhere, but if it's at all possible, I'd prefer my movements not to become public knowledge."

"Are you in trouble, Dad? I realise it's got to be the war, but—"

"No, son. I've been careful so far, but I may be extremely busy with things I can't tell you about just yet. All I can say is, this is my home country now, has been for over twenty years since I met your mother. I'd never do anything you'd be ashamed of or hate me for, but the less you know, the less you can let slip, even by accident. Do you understand?"

"Your word's good enough for me, Dad. How far might you be travelling? Will you need your passport?"

Frank smiled. "Not much gets past you does it, Lars? Yes, I can tell you that much, I think. You've a right to know where the old man's gone off to. Let's just say, certain people have asked me to help them with my language skills. I've taught you to speak German as it's spoken in Munich, and correctly pronounced Oxford English. You'll find these invaluable assets, I suspect. You're a talented musician, and the world really *could* be your oyster. I just hope I've prepared you for that possibility as well as I can.

"This coming weekend I *do* need to go to Copenhagen on genuine music school business. We're short of manuscript paper again, and I could do with some extra violin strings and clarinet reeds, though it's not certain I can find them. I might not be coming back immediately, but if I don't get back before Sunday evening, I'll get a message to you somehow. Ella Hansen's already agreed to cover my lessons on Monday, and that gives me an extra day before anyone needs to know I'm...not where everyone thinks I am. It's important that you keep up the charade for as long as possible if I'm not here. Okay?"

"Sure thing, Dad. You can rely on me."

"I know that, son. I just wish I could let you know more, but it's too big a risk for everyone concerned."

In the soundproofed room, the creaking and crackling of the bones in Frank's wiry frame as he stood to indicate the end of the confidential pow-wow was disturbingly loud.

"You're getting old, Dad!" Lars teased him as they left and retired to the rooms they kept for their private use.

"Never so old, I can't catch you to thump sense into your head when you need it," Frank replied, slinging his arm around his son's shoulders. "I'm glad we had this chat: it might not be necessary, but I'd much rather be honest with you. I'll sleep better tonight, that's for sure."

\* \* \*

From: Savage Canary
To: Chicken Shack
Code: Highest Security

Confirmed report (eyewitnesses) from Region VIII of TWO (2) U-boats travelling north via Store Bælt towards Kattegat. No known targets in the area. Objective not known. Information only. Local eyes on full alert.

When the War Planning Office transferred, bell, book and ring file from London to a fresh location beneath commercial property in Liverpool's docklands, security was so tight that even Martin's bank, which continued to serve the public above ground, was not immediately aware of its new subterranean neighbours. It was almost three months before the bank was informed that the underground tenants were 'a Government department'. Following this admission, every employee was offered the choice of signing the Official Secrets Act or spending the remainder of the war in an intern camp. There were no exceptions: everyone signed.

Within a fortnight, a separate, discreet entrance had been cut through from the Water Street entrance of the Merseyside underground train system, for the exclusive use of War Office employees. By spreading start and finish times over a twenty-four-hour period, it was possible to avoid having large numbers of staff arriving or leaving at specific times, while at the same time making for maximum efficiency, dealing with intelligence reports as they came in.

"Signal from Savage Canary. Who thought up the title 'Chicken Shack'?"

"That'll be Eastern Ops. The Canary's been quiet for a while, but all his intel has been good, and he seems to have a finger on everything going on throughout Scandinavia."

"That's a lot of territory!"

"Get that up to Peter Yates right away."

"On it!"

# Chapter Four

05050550
Condition: Black
Kdt *U-534*, eyes only
Highest Security
Read, Memorise, Destroy

0z, above date you will proceed to coordinates 080580 at optimum speed allowing for weather conditions and other vessels. Assume command over support vessels *U-3523* & *U-3503* if they are present. Do *not* under any circumstances delay departure if for any reason either or both vessels are NOT on station at 0600z.

At that location a surface vessel will initiate contact with you using a sequence which you will enter on the cryptograph supplied for your present mission. The code must translate as CORMORANT. Be prepared to abort operation if there is the slightest element of doubt re: identification. If security is compromised, you are to scatter and take independent evasive action. *U-3523* and *U-3503* are to be sacrificed if necessary:

**ced*U-534* must NOT under any circumstances fall into enemy hands, with or without the Highest Security cargo.**

You will transfer the three [3] items of cargo that were taken on board at Lübeck, together with ONE [1] of the Enigma cryptographic processors to the surface vessel which awaits you. Once transfer is complete, you will disengage immediately. If all three U-boats are present, you will disperse and return to the Fatherland independent of each other. Caution should be your paramount concern rather than speed of action. It is assumed that the CO of each U-boat will navigate, and that the location chosen for the handover of cargo remains unknown to the rest of each crew.

Heil Hitler
03maj45

\*\*\*

Herbert Nollau read the precise, unambiguous Order of the Day for perhaps the tenth time. It made no difference: the orders were unmistakable and crystal clear. There was no latitude for possible interpretation or prevarication, no way he might be able to 'duck and weave' as a sop to his conscience.

*No latitude.* The phrase echoed in his brain, reminding him of an outstanding task. Although he knew full well that he was alone and not under observation from any member of his crew, he held himself ramrod-straight and (apparently, at least) in full control as he turned to the map cabinet and ran a well-manicured fingernail across the spine of several charts until he found what he needed.

"Oh-eight-oh east, Five-eight-oh north," he murmured, placing the large, transparent T-square over the map. Without undue haste, he secured it on the tracking bar and positioned it to correspond with the coordinates he had been given.

The coordinates identified a point off the coast of Norway, with perhaps 200 metres of water under his keel.

A comfortable depth for hiding, and also for flight, he decided. The map showed an archipelago of small, uninhabited islands, few of which were dignified with a name: he assumed those that were named were the only ones upon which a brave handful of loners had decided to settle. Two named fjords carved their way into the mainland: one due west and the other slightly northeast of the position toward which he had been ordered to head.

He inspected the chart in detail. That particular section of the North Sea seabed appeared relatively clutter-free; rack his brain though he might, he could not recall any significant number of aerial battles having been fought in the area, though that didn't mean a great deal, as there was little reason for him to keep track of the skirmishes playing out every day in areas of the European arena that did not concern him and his vessel. All the same, he wouldn't need to take this particular large-scale map with him back to the central command post. He rolled it into its cylinder and replaced it on the rack. As he left the room, he made sure all the lights were out and the door was securely locked. On a submarine, there was no such thing as a reasonable margin of error, right down to the unnecessary power drain of a single light bulb left on in an empty room: the security breach which might follow from failure to close the door of a room containing classified information was unacceptable.

On returning to the con, he used the bosun's pipe to summon the whole crew by delivering three short blasts. He permitted off-duty crew the luxury of sufficient time to dress before issuing the set of instructions and orders he had planned. He was pleased to note that all fifty-one members of the crew were present in the overcrowded central area in considerably less than the three minutes he had allowed them in case some had been asleep.

"Prepare for a further round of sea trials. We will be running silent and deep, and pushing our engines to the limit.

I hope to achieve an average speed in excess of thirty knots while remaining as close to the seabed as is practical. We have received fresh instructions to meet with a German vessel some distance from here, and we will be running silent all the way. Be extremely conscious of any sudden, sharp noises such as a dropped tool, and keep conversations to a minimum. I have been given a set of coordinates for our destination. I will take the helm myself, to maintain the highest possible level of security."

"That is all. Prepare for silent running. I have the con."

Oberleutnant—soon to be Kapitänleutnant—Nollau had a reputation for running a tight, well-disciplined ship, but he achieved this without being an overbearing, dictatorial officer. U-534 was his first command, and he had received his commission as her first commanding officer as soon as she left dry dock, overseeing her sea trials before signing her off as a fully functional VII-C U-boat with extra modifications that dramatically increased her underwater speed and range.

Although fully armed and ready for action, she had completed her sea trials without the opportunity to engage the enemy, and this rankled with Nollau. He drilled his complement of crew constantly and efficiently and inspired a team spirit that was almost unknown in the German navy. He also developed a system of hand signals, which he insisted his crew learn and use instead of voiced orders and instructions, particularly under silent running conditions: effectively, any crew member unable to see the commander from his work station could relay a message by hand through only *one* intermediary. Communication was almost instantaneous and as accurate as any verbal chain of command.

Within ten minutes of him giving the order to prepare for silent running, every man was at his station and fully prepared for action. A further ten minutes were taken up by running through a checklist of over one hundred points he had decided were vital for operational efficiency; by the time

Nollau had completed his preparations, there was less than half an hour left for their escort vessels to reach the agreed rendezvous or alternatively send word to confirm they would either be delayed or otherwise prevented from taking part in the mission.

*That assumes that they have not been either captured or sunk,* Nollau thought as he made a brief note in his log and frowned at the unworthy thought. Had not the *Führer* himself promised that victory was inevitable, that they could look forward to a Reich which would last a thousand years? Surely at the very least he could expect the commanders of *U-3523* and *U-3505* to break radio silence long enough to confirm their continued existence.

Ten seconds before the sweep hand of his watch reached the figure 12 on the dial, he made a final note on the relevant page in his logbook, recording the fact that neither support vessel had contacted him before 0600z, and that he was therefore proceeding to his assigned objective alone.

He grasped the handles of the periscope exactly as the second hand passed its northernmost point: a final 360° sweep of the horizon was performed, accompanied by a single maximum strength *Ping!* on the sonar. One minute's grace was allowed, but when it produced no reaction, Nollau gave the hand signal which meant 'dive stations'. The powerful electric motors keened in unison, cycling upwards and just beyond the range of even the most sensitive of human ears. Nollau dipped *U-534*'s nose to his predetermined optimum cruising depth and cycled the engines up to full power. For a few minutes, every crew member felt a certain amount of discomfort before his body accustomed itself to the slight but definite increase in pressure experienced via the membranes in their eardrums.

*U-534* was many things that comparable Class VII craft were not. She was not designed as a hunter by nature, but nobody would have known that from a casual visual inspection. For example, the range (and, significantly, the *gross weight*) of the weaponry on board was minimal. *U-534* was not intended as an assault or attack vessel but for clandestine operations for which stealth and speed would be more important considerations. Being far lighter than others of similar size and engine power gave her a distinct edge when it came to speed and manoeuvrability.

Benzedrine tablets, strong coffee and the fear of a verbal lashing from the CO kept the crew on their toes for the two hours it took them to close in on their meeting point. Nollau throttled back and cruised at just above stalling speed as he approached the point at which his dead reckoning told him their meeting should be taking place. He knew, however, that they had arrived a good three hours early, and the last thing he wanted to do was draw attention to himself.

"Still no contact, Sir."

Nollau acknowledged the sonar operative's report with a curt nod. *Bloody amateurs*, he thought. *This is my first real command posting: I must therefore assume that they have more experience than I do, so why aren't they here on time?*

He plotted a minute cross indicating their exact position and pencilled the time next to it. His sonar screen had an underwater range of up to fifty kilometres, but there had been no activity to suggest the presence of any other underwater vessel as *U-534* had approached the rendezvous.

He looked at his watch and made an instant decision. It would be foolish to continue without risking a sweep of the immediate vicinity. If, for any reason, *U-3523* had been forced to surface, they might be under attack and require assistance. *U-3503* was coming from a separate mission and was not expected to join the wolfpack until they were much closer to their final destination, about twenty kilometres north of his present position.

"Take her up, but slowly," he muttered and glued himself to the periscope.

At a depth of five metres below the surface, he signalled a stop and sent up a flotation buoy with a radio antenna, which he decided was small enough to avoid observation: the more powerful single sonic *'ping'* this made possible was worth the risk. Thirty seconds later, having received no reply, he chanced a single 360° sweep. The sea was moderate, the horizon at least ten kilometres, and there were no surface vessels in sight.

Another hand signal—'dive stations'—and the fact that it was a hand signal, naturally, meant silent running conditions until further notice.

Nollau took the helm and indicated he wanted the bridge cleared before he entered the eyes-only coordinates he had taken from the Orders of the Day: 11°48′E 56°39′N.

Course would be a few points east of north: a final glance at the sonar confirmed that they were unlikely to encounter enemy shipping, as there was no activity on screen. Running at depth, they would remain unseen by aircraft. A check on average depths told him that he could run deep and silent with more than 150 metres under his keel, which he judged sufficient. They had almost an hour to reach the agreed coordinates: it seemed straightforward, but Herbert Nollau was not one to assume anything.

05050650 On station, coordinates as logged.

Nollau made the entry, then cautiously extended his periscope to clear the waterline from its maximum operating depth. If there were any sign of enemy shipping, he had to be prepared for a crash dive. On the other hand, if the generals and admirals had all their ducks in a row then the only surface craft in sight would be the one sent by High Command to meet them.

*A full 360° sweep: nothing in sight. Am I the only person left on the planet still fighting this war?* he wondered to himself wearily and not for the first time that month—or even that day if he were to be honest.

A second, slower sweep of the empty expanse of sea on all sides, quartering carefully, making sure that no detail, however small, could slip by unobserved. He had scanned clockwise from the north as far as about seven o'clock, where there was a smudge on the absolute limit of his range. Checking the charts, he breathed a sigh of relief: it could only be the Danish island, Anholt. There had been a British force there early in the war, but they had been targeted by the SS *Ostmark*, and had ceased to be a threat, according to reports.

*Still, better to be safe.* He continued his sweep, then froze. *What was that?* A glint of reflection as the sun struggled over the horizon and slung its first rays low over the sea… low over the dark haze of the island and invisible but for the low angle of the sun, a speck of something rapidly devolved into three specks of something, growing larger and becoming identifiable as the shapes of three aircraft.

It was surely too far from any base for them to be Luftwaffe, and he thought it most unlikely their mission—despite the enhanced security implied—qualified for air support. Still, discipline ruled, and he automatically made the silent hand signal for 'crash dive' rather than risk a radio broadcast on the U-boat's PA.

He watched carefully until the last second as the periscope slipped beneath the waves: the three dots had hardened to the outline of three aircraft, low on the horizon, thundering at wave height as they passed the dark smudge he'd already identified as the island of Anholt but still too far away to be recognised. He put *U-534*'s nose down and ran her electric motors up to maximum drive, easing off as she responded and headed cleanly for the maximum depth. Slowly, he forced himself to count under his breath, "A thousand and one, a thousand and two…" to keep some sort of check on the passing seconds while watching his sonar screen like a hawk. Three dots in a line crossed his screen from the south. As they passed the centre of the screen, he gestured for full revs from the port engine and swung the helm, locking his forearm muscles until they bulged, to make a swift 90° turn. As soon as she passed 50°, he signalled for the starboard engine, and by the time both engines were running at full throttle he was away, feinting east, intending to cut back and run nor-nor-west towards the original rendezvous point. He didn't like the way the three planes—which he had to assume were Allied Forces, this far from any Luftwaffe base—had seemed to be heading straight towards his position even before they cleared Anholt, as if they knew where to find him.

As long as he could maintain his present depth, he thought he could escape detection from any casual overflight. His charts were of recent vintage, but experience had taught him that not all wreckage had been reported and recorded during the last few months of the war, and he was in effect running blind, possibly depending on charts which were dangerously out of date.

At the edge of his screen, a comfortable distance to his west, three ducks lined up, and he knew that the same planes had turned and were beating back along the return path. Whether they'd dropped depth charges or simply overflown the narrow channel separating Denmark from Sweden on a routine reconnaissance mission was now academic: they hadn't had him in their sights after all. His trigger finger itched: if he'd been on the surface and with even the minimum standard deck guns for a Class VII U-boat, he was certain he'd have picked them off. *U-534*, however, had been designed for other missions, stripped of all the usual heavy artillery and a lot of the armour—the price which had to be paid for increased speed, range and manoeuvrability.

He eased his nose up a fraction and cut back the throttle, intending to drift slowly closer to the surface without attracting undue attention: the danger, it seemed, was past, the enemy returning to base after a long sortie, presumably short of fuel.

The mud and the sand of the sea bottom around him exploded in a frighteningly soundless cauldron of flash and a pressure wave, which ripped the helm from his hands and sent the second officer flying. After a second's utter blackness, the emergency lighting came on, and a warning klaxon began to howl.

"Kill that!" he snapped into the PA horn; radio silence was no longer of any use to him or his crew. He was gratified, nonetheless, when the order was obeyed immediately. "Damage report by sectors—Sector Six, stern?"

"Moderate—leaking too fast to pump."

"Evacuate—schnell!

"Section Five, Section Four: evacuate immediately three men to a hatch, all hatches port and starboard nine through twenty. In thirty seconds, I dive. You have this one chance for an easy exit!

"Section Three, report."

There were a few unidentifiable noises. Then:

"Severe damage—"

Nollau cut in. "Evacuate, hatches on both flanks, three men to a hatch. You have to make about thirty metres for the surface. I will delay final dive as long as possible!

"Section Two, hear this. Evacuate using all means. We are now holding at twenty metres depth and you should make it. Good luck.

"Anyone still with me in Section One should have left when ordered to do so almost five minutes before the attack took place. Report to torpedo room if you are still in Section One. That is all. A captain goes down with his ship. *Heil Hitler!*"

The whipcrack of the familiar phrase—not part of Herbert Nollau's daily vocabulary—produced the intended effect, a weak but determined response from his second officer, whom he knew was still in Section 1 but had no way of knowing whether or not he was conscious, and a muttered cadence from the sonar operator, whose presence he had forgotten about.

"Quickly, now! I can trim her to hold at this depth, but if we're to evacuate, we need to close off the torpedo bay! Run!"

Nollau half-carried the sonar operator into the bay and spun the door closed. He forced the SO—hardly more than a boy, really—to look him in the eye.

"From this depth, you have to trust me. It's twenty metres to the surface, and you have to breathe OUT slowly as you swim to the surface, or your lungs will explode from the pressure. Do you understand?"

The boy looked at him and nodded slowly.

"Good! It will be a miracle if we all make it alive, but as far as I'm aware, we've taken no casualties yet. Into the tube, and I'll fire it off. Take a good breath as soon as the door slams!"

Without giving the child soldier a chance to think about it, Herbert Nollau boosted him up into the tube and slammed the door. A split second later he hit the 'fire' button and heard the *crump!* as the charge propelled the sailor out of the tube.

He took a second to assess the state of mind of his number two.

"Dieter, I won't try to fool you. You know as well as I do that the chances of this working are no better than fifty-fifty, but I have to try."

"Rubbish, Herbert! I'll see you on your usual seat in the *Reeperbahnen* before the end of the month, and if not there, we'll show 'em all how to celebrate when we meet again in the halls of Valhalla!"

Dieter snatched a flat, uninflated life jacket from a stash in the corner and threw it into Torpedo Tube 3 before crawling in behind it. Seeing there was still enough space, Nollau packed a second jacket snugly behind his friend's feet before slamming the door.

"*Schuss, mein bruder!*" was all he could think of as his fist slammed down once more on the trigger and the craft rocked very slightly from the pressure charge.

Despite his final speech to the whole of his crew, Herbert Nollau did *not* intend to go down with his ship, dying a lonely death from drowning or a longer and more painful death from starvation. His orders were quite specific. After dealing with his entire crew, he was to use Torpedo Tube 2 to effect his own escape. This tube had been specially fitted to allow for it to be detonated by someone crouching *inside* it and riding a rocket to salvation.

On opening Torpedo Tube 2, Nollau froze for a moment in shock. Already installed in the tube was one of the three highest security cargo items, which had been transferred to U-534 at their first open-sea rendezvous point. Stripped of almost all its protective packing, it was clearly a weapon, perhaps twelve or fifteen feet in length, secured with polystyrene foam cuffs at both ends and in the centre. It was wooden, and of great antiquity. The polystyrene cuffs meant that the spear itself was held securely, without coming into contact with the walls of the torpedo tube. There was adequate room for Nollau to curl part of his body alongside the tail, with his feet pressed against the closed torpedo tube door. The 'eject' button was exactly where his final orders told him it would be. He pressed it and held on for what promised to be either the ride of his life or a brief but spectacular sojourn on the highway to hell. Lungs full of air, he felt his ears pop with pressure as the gate opened and he was kicked forwards, his arms clamped to the spear-like object as it gathered pace and soared towards the pale promise of breathable air. Nollau closed his eyes and prayed.

# Chapter Five

"This is just in, Sir. The source is one which has always been reliable."

Warrant Officer 2$^{nd}$ Class Warren placed a single sheet of close-typed text on Brigadier Nolan's desk and stepped back, fully alert but in a recognised at-ease attitude, ready to stay or go as needed.

Brigadier Nolan nodded his acknowledgement of Warren's continued presence but made no attempt to dismiss his aide. His eyes darted back and forth as he read the signal through rapidly, then again more slowly…and even slower for a third time. With each reading, his brow furrowed a little more.

"Action, Sir? Do you want me to bring anyone else in on this?"

Invitations were invariably delivered by word of mouth rather than in writing or by telephone, for the highest possible security.

"Top brass Navy will have to be here. This is their department."

"Captain Johnny Walker's on leave, Sir."

"Top of the list. I'll want someone familiar with the Eastern Front, too. And see if you can find me a couple of linguists. This contact seems to be comfortable with English, but the message comes from Denmark and we may need some assistance."

"Is there anyone with security clearance at the Scandinavian church?"

"I know the Pastor, Ole Jerg. One of their Free Fighters had to pancake with a damaged plane about a week ago, and Ole contacted his squadron for us. We can rely on him, I'm sure, and he's fluent in all the Scandinavian languages, which is a plus!"

"Anyone else?"

Brigadier Nolan looked through his contacts list.

"Baltic ops: Commander Yates, or someone from his immediate staff. Let's keep it as simple as possible for now. We don't want to start a panic by bringing in too many people. It has to be kept low profile until we know more."

Warren was already on his way. The main advantage of 'keeping it simple' was the fact that most of the day-to-day operations could be achieved without the need for written notes, which were regarded as a potential security risk. Verbal messages were preferred and, by and large, were quicker and more efficient.

\*\*\*

Ole Jerg paused outside the anonymous door with a corroded brass plate which read 'Staff'. Before taking the key out of his pocket, he glanced in both directions along the passage sloping down from Water Street to the underground station: there was nobody else in sight.

As he closed the door softly, he was met by a young lady in naval trim. She held a clipboard and was clearly expecting visitors.

"Your ID, please?"

It was said with a smile, but Ole noted how this smartly dressed young lady had avoided the trap of assuming he was entitled to the traditional priest's cravat he was wearing and sidestepped the need to add either 'Sir' or 'Pastor/Reverend' at the end of her greeting. He was impressed by this minute attention to detail.

While she was looking at his papers, he swung his topcoat off and folded it over his left arm. The manner in which it seemed to flow through the air and settle into a neatly folded garment was not entirely due to excellent bespoke tailoring. It was just as much a result of the even weight distribution caused by the creation of discreet concealed 'poacher pockets' of varying sizes in the lining of the garment. Ole had travelled rather more than would be expected of the majority of SKU priests during the past five years, ostensibly receiving instruction from the bishops in Copenhagen, Stockholm and Oslo. In reality, he was the main contact between the British Home Office and the Resistance movements in the three Scandinavian countries. Until now, he had never been questioned on a journey. When asked about how he got through every checkpoint without any problems, his instinctive (if naïve) reaction was to ask, "Who'd think to challenge a priest?"

His general appearance was also an asset of sorts: he was a big man, towering over six foot and close to three hundred and fifty pounds, with a snow-white mane and beard, which he referred to as his inbuilt protection against the bitter winters of northern Scandinavia. This left little more than his piercing blue eyes and scarred, not-quite-straight nose as his most compelling visual features.

"People say, 'Fat boy, can't run!'" he would joke in apparent self-mockery. The fact remained that even if he was almost as wide around the hips as he was tall, he had yet to be stopped and searched at any border control in Europe.

Whether it was coincidence or the natural defences of an animal accustomed to being hunted, some instinct made Ole step to one side a fraction of a second before the sound of a key in the door behind him, which burst open to reveal an old-young face with a neatly trimmed beard and dark navy-blue jacket with a captain's insignia on the sleeve and collar. Almost perched on the crown of his head was a cap, which was most definitely not set at an admiralty-approved angle.

"Morning, Ole!"

"Captain Johnny! Sunk any U-boat fleets recently?"

Johnny Walker's successes in a long-running battle with U-boats attacking Atlantic convoys bringing vital raw materials from the US to England had been a major news item for some time.

He shook Ole's hand in greeting, but his eyes flicked to a wall poster, one of a series of public information posters reminding the general population of the sad fact that 'Careless Talk Costs Lives'. Ole took the hint and turned to the female orderly who was acting as receptionist.

"Is Commander Yates here yet?"

She hesitated as if deliberating whether an answer—affirmative or otherwise—could be construed as a security breach.

Brigadier Nolan noticed her discomfort and came to her aid.

"He arrived a few minutes before you and went ahead. Corporal, if you'll escort our guests, I'll be right behind you."

"Yes, Sir! Please follow me, gentlemen."

She led them a short distance along a corridor painted in approved MoD colours; Brigadier Nolan, with three or four slim folders under his arm, brought up the rear. They stopped at a door which had neither nameplate nor number to identify it. It contained a spartan working desk furnished with a telephone. Basic tea- and coffee-making facilities were on a side table, next to a rack of charts and maps. One of the four chairs around the table was taken by Commander Peter Yates: he waved them to join him, and as soon as the corporal had closed the door, he began, without preamble.

"We have received a signal from a source which has, so far, proved reliable." He distributed three carbon copies of the flimsy telegraph skin he was holding. "I got it thirty minutes ago. Looking at the DTG, it was sent at seventeen hundred Zulu time." He looked at his watch and frowned. How had it taken two hours for a high-priority signal to arrive?

As if reading his thoughts, Captain Walker spoke up. "They're on Daylight Saving, same as us, Sir. It's barely an hour ago this was sent."

"That's better, but still, look at the timing of it from the beginning. The initial sighting was early this morning!"

There was silence for a few moments while the four men around the table read the dispatch.

> DTG 05051700z – Savage Canary to Home Farm
>
> Activity Fehmarn Belt/East Sea/Kattegat reported, starting 0600z d.d.
>
> Two Dolphins entering Broad Belt, bearing NNE. Speed not confirmed, but suggests rendezvous planned, not routine patrol.
>
> Landmarks for possible rendezvous:
>
> Greenfjord (Norwegian waters)
>
> Anholt (Danish waters) currently unoccupied
>
> Læsø (Danish waters) Civilian residents, small GOP presence
>
> Message received: 05051812a

"Still, it's over twelve hours since the initial sighting, which seems to be just within German waters. Johnny, what sort of speed can a U-boat make?"

"If the skipper wants to push it, probably thirty knots underwater. Knock at least five off that if he has to surface, though."

"Let's assume he gets lucky. Once they're past Fyn and into Kattegat, there's little chance of him—or them, if they stay together—being spotted. There's no traffic in that region, and we'd get no particular tactical or military advantage from patrolling that particular sector. All three countries who share the waters are—officially, at least—neutral territory."

"We need confirmation, if possible."

Brigadier Nolan was already reaching for the nearest phone, glancing at Commander Yates for permission before dialling and receiving a tacit nod. Air ops were Brigadier Nolan's remit.

"War Office. Alert bases in NE England, scramble a flight—ideally at least three planes, long-range Spitfires—to carry out a reconnaissance mission over Norway and Sweden, exact target TBC within thirty minutes. Find out who is fuelled up and ready to go. Call Home Farm when you can confirm who's sending them up."

He replaced the handset and picked up the single sheet of information again. He shook his head and sighed.

"Not a lot to be going on, but the coordinates look promising. They're certainly better than the pure guesstimates we usually get!"

Commander Yates turned and pinned up a 10' x 4' nautical map of Kattegat, showing partial coastlines of Denmark, Norway and Sweden around the perimeter.

"You can see that any sea traffic coming from the south has to choose to pass this island, Fyn—" he tapped it with a pointer "—either east or west. The western channel is narrower and more difficult to pass without being observed, but a sub at night, in good hands—anything's possible, I suppose."

"And give credit where it's due," Johnny Walker muttered, "we know from experience that the Germans have kept some of their best skippers for the U-boats." It wasn't easy to admit it out loud, but it was a fact.

"How can our informant be certain there was more than one U-boat if all they saw was the wake?"

"The report comes from one of the local fishermen. He knows the waters like the back of his hand, he's fished the Østresø—I think that's right, Jerry calls it 'Ostersee'—for many years, and I think we can trust his judgement. If he says there was more than one vessel, the sensible thing is to build our response on a worst-case scenario. So, we assume two targets and plan accordingly."

Johnny Walker loped forwards from the back of the room and took charge of the pointer.

"Once they're north of Fyn, it gets considerably deeper as well as widening out. That's going to make even *one* U-boat harder to track. If they split up, it's going to mean two separate search patterns. Do we have any clues? Why are they heading north—*away* from home? What's up there which might be a worthwhile target?"

Brigadier Nolan flinched and turned to scrutinise the wall map more closely.

"Could be coincidence."

"But you don't believe in coincidences."

Johnny Walker dropped his comment into the awkward silence.

The brigadier nodded. "This isn't even official, but I can think of two possible targets."

"We've had reports this past week of a renewal of interest in the heavy water facility in Telemark."

"Hang on a minute!" Johnny Walked broke in. "Didn't the Specials sort that problem out about two years ago now? I thought they'd destroyed the place, literally!"

The brigadier looked at each of his advisors in turn, evidently deciding how much of what he knew he could reveal. He sighed, loosened his tie and undid his collar button.

"Gentlemen, this is going to be a long night. I suggest you make yourselves comfortable because I've no idea where and when you'll sleep next, and we'll be living on meals delivered to us in this office until further notice."

Johnny was already in an open-neck shirt, and it took Ole a one-second tug to remove his slightly anachronistic Scandinavian pastor's ruffed collar, a far more decorative and totally impractical badge of office than the simple dog collar worn by English vicars and priests.

Johnny Walker was first out of the blocks with a question. "Brigadier, I—"

"As we're going to be in each other's face for as long as this exercise lasts, perhaps we can dispense with titles? I'd much prefer to be just plain James for the duration. I can't remember the last time somebody used my Christian name."

Johnny grinned. "Suits me, James. And Commander Yates?"

"Peter suits me fine."

"All my family—and a fair number of my parishioners—call me Ole anyway, so I can't hide behind a title even if I wanted to, which, I have to say, I find irritating and almost invariably unnecessary in others."

"Except those who think they have something to hide, perhaps?" drawled Johnny, one leg slung up over the armrest of his chair.

"Well, I suppose there is always *that* sort of *necessary*—brought on by guilt!" Ole grinned, and the final few shards of ice which could have hindered the gelling of the group melted away at once.

"Right, we can agree to sod the formalities," said the brigadier. "Johnny, you were about to say?"

"Permission to smoke?" He already had a tin in his hand and a cigarette well on the way to fully rolled. He popped a match with his thumbnail without waiting for an answer and continued. "Any idea what class U-boat—or U-boats—we're hunting? Any way we can find out? It would help to learn anything at all about the target's capabilities, weaponry, range, complement of crew..."

Peter Yates scribbled a note and reached for his pipe. "Your experience and success in hunting U-boats are exactly what I wanted to bring to this table, Johnny," he said, approvingly. He picked up his phone and relayed Johnny Walker's supplementary questions to someone at the other end of a direct line, which his companions noted he didn't have to dial.

"Can't promise anything, but we'll just have to wait and see what they can dig up for us. Johnny, how would knowing any of this help us?"

"If they're older models, they'll be slower, less manoeuvrable, possibly less well armoured. The new Class Sevens are faster, have a much better range, and it's said they can run much longer underwater and on electric motors. Then there's the question of the full complement of the crew. That would make a hell of a difference if it comes to a stand-up, slug-it-out, toe-to-toe battle."

Peter Yates grinned. "I see why you've a reputation for careful planning in your sub-hunting missions!"

"Planning's the most important stage, if you want to avoid casualties," Johnny countered. He ground out his cigarette and drained his coffee cup, then stood, and with a typical rolling seaman's gait, he crossed the room to study the wallchart. "Let's assume two Class VII subs, the latest model we *know* of, with standard fittings—deck guns fore and aft, and four torpedo tubes, crew of fifty."

"Does that include the captain?" Ole asked. Johnny paused a moment, thought about it, and shook his head.

"Probably not. All right, let's say max fifty-one on each sub. There's a limit to how long they can run on canned air. They'd want to surface during hours of darkness to recharge their batteries, which would be under constant use in silent running, and take the opportunity of getting a breath of fresh air."

"Near as dammit midsummer. Depending on moon phases, and whether there's any significant cloud cover, there's quite a small window this far north." Peter Yates was immediately interested and flicked through his notes. "Here it is. Last quarter, 6th May at six-fifteen Zulu. The new moon's on 9th May and that's just before twenty-one thirty— it's as dark as it going to get, these next few nights, but only between…oh, let's say about two and five in the morning! Does that help?"

"Can we get a couple of Spitfires to overfly the area and take some recce shots? How good is our film for night photography?"

"We've got the planes and the pilots, no problems flying out of Newcastle or Durham, and the Eastern theatre has been relatively quiet for some time, so they won't be needed for defence either."

As the only non-military presence in the room, Ole Jerg was astonished at how quickly and efficiently decisions were made and orders expedited in the space of a hectic but controlled ten minutes or so of telephone calls. For him, it was like watching a well-drilled team going into action: all three experts seemed to know exactly who to contact and what to say. There was no need for raised voices, nor was there any repetition (as far as he could tell) which might have been caused by possible misunderstandings or queries from the people to whom the calls were made.

\* \* \*

## 2345z

Two long-range modified Spitfires with the latest developments in nocturnal photography on board took off from a small airfield outside Minehead. Just before midnight, they were joined over the North Sea by a Liberator long-range bomber flying out of King's Lynn. They were to provide escort and protection for the larger aircraft, which was virtually unable to defend itself: the Liberator's target was the remains of the heavy water plant at Telemark, in Norway.

Although the plant itself had been virtually destroyed in one of the most successful sabotage raids of modern times, the stockpiles of deuterium oxide had been left untouched, and intelligence reports suggested that Germany's High Command were planning to remove it, possibly to a research establishment deep within their own borders, where it could be developed into a potent nuclear weapon, providing they had obtained or could produce enough of the unstable compound.

The planes broke above cloud at ten thousand feet, and the Liberator pilot breathed a sigh of relief when it appeared that they had the skies to themselves. Norman Baker was no coward, but he was well aware of his plane's limited capabilities in a dogfight and eternally grateful for the presence of the Spitfires, which droned reassuringly, one on each wingtip.

His radio crackled, and he heard the calm voice of his port-side escort pilot.

"Fox, this is Vixen One. We have orders for a secondary objective. You have clear skies and zero, repeat, zero indication of bandits on our scopes. We have been given ninety-two megahertz as a secure radio wavelength. Confirm?"

"Fox to Vixen One, receiving loud and clear. What weather can we expect?"

"No change expected. However, we've one more game ploy, which the boffins at base tell me will confuse the hell out of Jerry. I'm told this trick might even cause an unexpected shower of rain from the clouds below us! Tally-ho, Corky!"

The escort Spitfires peeled away from the Liberator and sank into the clouds. As they did, they left behind them a trail which resembled the smoke of a misfiring engine and was only slightly denser than gas. It settled and floated for a moment on contact with the clouds before obeying the immutable law of gravity and sinking through the layers.

The continuous stream the two fighter planes left in their wake swiftly became miles long and gossamer thin. It consisted of hundreds of thousands of thin, feather-light strips of aluminium foil, which circled and spread and served only one purpose: to confuse and distract any hostile eyes that might have spotted an unexplained blip on their radar screen, allowing the Liberator and her escorts to continue their clandestine mission.

"Levelling out at two thousand feet. Stay in the clouds as long as poss, Corky."

"Roger that, Biffo. No point in advertising our presence."

"My instruments put us five minutes from the sector we want, on my mark...now!"

Mickey Corcoran noted the time and rapidly scanned the trip switches for the cameras fitted at strategic points fore and aft on the fuselage of his Supermarine Mark IV Spit. It was an identical twin in every respect with the plane flown by his squadron leader, Roy 'Biffo' Burton, armed to the teeth and equipped with the latest available cameras and supersensitive film, ideal for night shoots.

"Two minutes. Hold steady, heading two-nine-five degrees."

"Copy. Heading two-nine-five degrees," Mick chanted automatically, making the tiniest of unnecessary corrections to his helm as he spoke.

"Dive."

Throttling back close to the engine's tick-over speed induced an eerie hush which, after a couple of hours on full revs, seemed like a deafening silence. Now—for a few precious minutes, at least—gravity could do some of the final approach work as they stooped like a pair of hawks, not on power but still under the full, expert control of their respective pilots.

Biffo had memorised the important details of the area before take-off. He recognised the distinctive, triangular shape of the island on his starboard bow immediately he cleared the cloud base at just over one thousand feet.

"Anholt, two o'clock, Corky. You may be able to see some lights from a town called Grenå on your port wingtip."

"Affirmative. Want me to go round?"

"Negative. Follow me, we'll turn over open water—no point making a racket above Denmark. Start your cameras rolling before we go about, we've plenty of film! We might as well keep shooting until it's all gone—unless, of course, dear Uncle Adolf decides to chase us off before we're finished"

"Roger. Out."

Vixen One and Two circled lazily through a gentle arc between Frederikshavn and the island of Læsø before dropping their noses and picking up speed for a lightning run due south from the northern tip of the stretch of water known as the Kattegat. They'd only get one shot at this: even now, just as the sun was rising in the east, they were heading into one of the most densely populated regions along Sweden's west coast and Sjælland, the eastern half of Denmark. To get any degree of useable detail, they'd have to make a low pass, and it was not going to be possible to remain unseen. The only thing in their favour was the element of surprise.

"Tally-Ho!"

With the traditional hunting cry that had become part and parcel of the RAF's image, Biffo Burton dropped his nose and thrust the throttle fully open. Even with the engine bellowing at full throat, he could hear the rapid, steady rhythm of the camera shutters as they clicked, taking still shots, or whirred as they recorded moving images.

It was all too easy and over in seconds. Above the straits that separated Denmark from Germany, the two planes circled to face north once more. Below them, had they but known, Søren Jeppe glanced up from mending a net. His practised eye correctly identified the distinctive Spitfire silhouette, and his attention returned to repairing the tools of his trade.

Now they had revealed their presence, it was quite possible that this second pass was going to be more dangerous: it all depended on how swiftly the German ground forces could react, after being caught 'with their pants down' during the first pass.

"Bet Jerry's ringing round, trying to find out who we were strafing!" chuckled Biffo into his mic. His large frame had given rise to his nickname: he seemed to wear the cockpit as others would a carefully tailored overcoat.

"We shouldn't disappoint him. Let's give 'em a few rounds to be thinking about on the return trip!" suggested Micky.

"Sorry, Corky, not this time! There's too much at stake, and we haven't got half the holiday snaps in the can yet! This is a recce mission, remember, *not* a raid! But maybe we can go looking for the *shoals of herring* in the North Sea, on our last lap, *after* we've got the pictures! Will that satisfy your blood lust?"

"Mmm, gore, Igor!" growled Mick, parodying the Ealing Studios school of horror movies. "That's a Roger, Captain. Ready on your mark!"

"Mark!"

Again, the identical twins came thundering over Store Bælt, but this time at little more than wavetop level. Biffo had calculated that there was little chance of being fired upon from any land-based artillery, and their southbound flight scant minutes earlier had confirmed that there were no bogeys in the channel separating Sjælland from the remainder of Denmark. The cameras were working overtime again as they reached maximum velocity and levelled out for sustained, steady shots.

"Coming up on Anholt. I'm breaking east, over Swedish airspace."

"Roger, Captain. I'll bank west, over Skagen."

"Switch to ninety-two megahertz. It's time we contact the Fox and escort him home."

"Copy that, Captain. Switching channels."

From the corner of his eye, as he reached to change channels in Vixen One, Biffo sensed rather than saw a suggestion of a shape, too regular to be a natural subsurface rock formation. The hairs on the back of his neck rose as the predator instinct that had made him a leading scorer in confirmed kills kicked in.

"We can come back this way. It won't even be a detour if we're escorting him to King's Lynn," he promised himself. He then spent a whole ten seconds calculating how long it might take them to rendezvous with the slower, more vulnerable Liberator and return to this approximate area, and tossed in a random figure to allow for how far a sub—more specifically, a Class Seven U-boat—might travel in, say, two hours. "Over and Out."

He was barely aware of tagging the familiar phrase to the end of his previous sentence. Radio silence wasn't just good practice; it had become vital to every fighter pilot's chances to survive and fight another day.

He drew alongside Corky in Vixen Two, then silently pointed to the clouds massing a few hundred feet above their heads. His silent signal was understood: Corky gave a thumbs up and peeled off left as Biffo banked right. Even flying blind or on instruments alone, they were both confident they could be close to the point at which they had left the Liberator in order to carry out their own special mission.

As they shrugged off the blanket of cloud and emerged into full daylight, Biffo looked at his watch. Barely forty minutes had passed since they had parted from the Liberator: had this given the bomber pilot enough time to wreak whatever mischief he had planned? As he pondered this, a faint *blip* appeared on his radar screen, heading straight towards him. He toggled the radio switch.

"Vixen One to Fox Leader."

The response was immediate.

"This is Fox Leader. I have two, repeat two, birds on my screen, bearing due east and closing on my position. Over."

"Fox Leader, I can confirm you are on my screen. We are approaching. Rendezvous with you at angels fifteen, approximate ETA five minutes."

"Negative, Vixen One. I've taken a hit, cannot risk that altitude. Request rendezvous *below* cloud level, *circa* angels two."

Under his breath, Biffo swore. Escorting a damaged bomber over several hundred miles of open sea without being able to hide in or above the security of cloud cover was not going to be easy.

*First things first!* he thought to himself and toggled the talk switch once more. "Received and understood, Fox Leader. Rendezvous below cloud base. The cupboard's bare at the moment."

This was a reference to the lack of other air traffic on his radar screens, made in a deliberately obtuse fashion as a precaution against German eavesdroppers sifting the invisible ether for radio signals, which could make their remaining journey hazardous.

Biffo cut the radio and glanced to his left, where Corky flew in tight formation, almost at his wingtip. A wag of the wing and a thumbs-down signal was enough: they both trimmed their noses into a steep dive, peeling away from each other and plunging into the clouds to take up the rearranged rendezvous altitude.

Biffo broke free of the clouds and quickly scanned the skies. He breathed a sigh of relief as he saw that they apparently had the skies to themselves. In the middle distance, west of his position, was a coastal city which could only be Gothenburg.

"Vixen Two, circle south. I will circle north and meet you east—that should place us behind Fox Leader and make it easier to rendezvous with him if he's sustained significant damage."

"Roger, Vixen One. Should we play hide-and-seek in the cloud base?"

"Affirmative. Sweden is officially neutral, but we may get some ack-ack over a major town."

A light touch on the joystick was all that was needed to re-enter the concealment of the clouds. Both pilots were accustomed to instrument flying: they flew straight and level for almost five minutes, heading due east.

"Vixen Two, time to go home. Circle clockwise, set altimeter at two thousand feet."

"Roger, Vixen One. Altimeter at two thousand. Meet you there, over."

"Over and Out."

Toggling the 92 MHz radio channel once more, Squadron Leader Burton made what he hoped would be the last radio transmission necessary.

"Vixen One to Fox Leader. Descending to angels two. Expect two marks on your radar, approaching from east, over."

The response was immediate and reassuring.

"Fox Leader calling. I have two approaching on my screen. You are exactly where I expected you to be. Well done!"

"Copy that, Fox Leader. We'll close in and escort you. Have you assessed the damage to your plane? Over."

"Rear gunner has sustained a slight injury. He reports some damage to our tail. My rudder's not responding but she's flyable. I'm going to dump excess ballast over the North Sea. I don't want to land with a full rack of depth charges."

"Fox Leader, I have you on visual. We're right behind you, coming on station—mark!"

Biffo throttled back to match speed with the lumbering shape of the Liberator, and Corky slotted into a similar position on the bomber's port flank Thumbs up all round was enough to confirm that the pilot of the bomber had seen them. The edges of the tail fin were somewhat ragged, but there was no evidence of oil leakage or engine damage. After a swift exchange of hand signals, the three planes descended to under three hundred feet and the Liberator released his unwanted cargo where the only damage it could do was make a temporary difference to the fish population in the immediate vicinity.

Remembering the unexplained shadow he'd noticed on the outward leg, Biffo checked how much of the surveillance film was left in the can. Enough, he decided, and hit the record button.

"Corky, blow off whatever film you've got left. I'll explain later, back at base, but I saw something odd on the way out, just north of Anholt…"

# Chapter Six

"Jim, about that message from the Danish Resistance group..."

"Yes, Ole, go on."

"Looks as though we've got a confirmation...of sorts."

Although Ole had worked alongside Peter Yates and Johnny Walker several times, Brigadier Nolan's fastidious attention to detail and his insistence on wearing full parade-ground dress uniform every day made him something of an unknown quantity. Jim looked up sharply.

"We've always had good intel from the Savage Canary. He's been one of our best operatives throughout this conflict. But you said confirmation, so who's it from?"

Ole took a telegraph flimsy from a slim wallet containing no more than three or four sheets: it would almost certainly be overstuffed and bulging before they went home at the end of their shift.

"It's from the Spitfire escort detailed to protect a Liberator from King's Lynn on a special last night. They all got back safely this morning, and the two Spits have some very interesting film footage they'd like us to look at. Some movie film, some stills."

"Let's see it, then."

Without further ado, Jim dimmed the lights, and all four team members swung their chairs to face the combined whiteboard and film screen. There was no soundtrack, and the pictures were a slightly grainy black-and-white, but they were clear enough for the purpose. In the bottom-right corner of each still, there was a DTG to identify when the shot had been taken. A similar message was superimposed at regular intervals on the cine film.

"First pass, the Spits were ordered to do some recon while they were over the area anyway. A message from a Resistance group in Region Eight alerted us to some unusual activity, subs—U-boats, rather—running silent and deep, coming up from the south, destination unknown. Here, the leader plane's got them *both* in his sights as they sneak up from the Baltic, approaching Fyn."

A succession of shots showed two lozenge shapes diverging from each other, evidently intending to make a break for it by passing Fyn, one to the east, the other by the narrower, more dangerous channel to the west.

"No reports of discovery west of Fyn?"

This from Johnny Walker. His unlit roll-up and the murderous silence when a shake of the head was the only response to his question were sufficient to indicate his opinion of the laxity this indicated—to him, at least.

"How about later footage? Anything which shows they met up again north of Fyn? Or did they go their separate ways? I wonder. After all, *our* flyboys were on two different missions. It was pure chance they were heading in more or less the same direction *and* at a time which made it possible for them to link up and protect each other."

"Nothing rock solid, not what I'd call proof, I'm afraid." Brigadier Yates said it so cheerfully, it sounded almost insincere, and his three companions stared at him. He advanced the frame-by-frame stills footage this time.

"This was taken about an hour later, as they return from their escort detail over Sweden and Norway, but that was a separate mission. If it becomes relevant, I can fill you in on what you need to know later on. But this recon was the main purpose of the Spits being scrambled, and as far as we can tell, there would only seem to be the one bogey in the water at this point. We have to assume that the other vessel was delayed, or developed problems."

"I haven't heard of what might be termed the ultimate problem—being sunk," Johnny grunted, relighting his cigarette as he spoke.

"No, there's been no activity reported at all," Jim confirmed. "The Danish sector of the North Sea has been completely free of reported traffic for some time. In fact, it's almost as if Jerry's given up contesting that particular arena."

"Logical enough, if you're losing hand over fist in other areas," Pete chipped in. "We've certainly bloodied his nose for him in Africa, for starters!"

"Yes, well, let's not get too carried away," Johnny Walker interrupted. "A lot of the scuttlebutt doing the rounds is just that—unconfirmed rumours." As the only group member who had been in the Middle East recently, he spoke with a degree of authority.

Jim Nolan was silent, engrossed in the still photographs: he plucked out three frames which had caught his interest. "The DTGs are very similar. I'm guessing they're consecutive, or very close?"

There were thirty seconds between one pair, and the third was taken within a minute of the first. A dark shadow could be seen clearly, dead centre in the first photograph. It was too regular to be a natural rock feature or any similar structure. From the angle of the shot, it had been taken from an acute, low angle as the Spitfire approached it.

"Can you tighten up the magnification? Are we seeing it from astern, or is he coming *towards* us—I mean, towards the camera on the plane?"

Johnny Walker picked up a magnifying glass. "You can just about make out the suggestion of a *Vee* in the foreground—here." He used the loupe's shadow on the screen to point out the detail he'd spotted. It was faint, but once the expert sub-hunter had pointed it out, it was without doubt evidence of the passage of a vessel.

"Sooo, she was heading north when this was taken?" Pete speculated.

"Correct. Are these the coordinates, up in the left-hand corner? Thought so!"

In seconds, Johnny had stuck a pin in the wall map of the stretch of water known as the Kattegat. He did it so calmly and with such self-assurance that none of his colleagues blinked an eye. His reputation was such that nobody expected him to make mistakes.

"Now, Jim, can you overlay the flight paths the Liberator used out and back? Great!"

After a minor miracle of *legerdemain*, which adjusted the second set of figures to show on the same scale as the overview of the Kattegat, Johnny called for—and was given—the flight path used by the Spitfires from Minehead to their rendezvous over the North Sea with the vulnerable bomber plane.

"Has this got any planning value?" Pete asked. "Could we use it to work out what they *might* do next?"

Johnny tapped his teeth with a pencil. "Maybe. Let's see now..." For a few seconds, he busied himself covering most of a page with mathematical symbols. Eventually, he raised his head. "Briefly, the answer is, yes!" He laid his notepad aside and made the points he felt he needed to make with his hands alone. "It looks to me as though he's headed north, towards Varberg on the west coast of Sweden—unless he's chancing his arm and heading for Gothenburg. That would be a major target..."

"But?"

"But it's too heavily defended, Peter. It would be downright suicide for a single U-boat. No commander would ever entertain the idea, even if he were to get his orders direct from Adolf himself!"

"What's at Varberg?"

"Nothing of any military or tactical value, as far as we're aware."

Jim rubbed both hands over his face. It had been a long session, in a closed room with no ventilation, which had become distinctly stale with tobacco smoke. "On the whole, I think it more likely they're heading for a rendezvous somewhere at sea."

"And the next question: with whom, and for what purpose?"

"I think that's the crux of the matter, Johnny. If I had to make a guess…" Jim paused for a moment and stared into space. "I'd say she'll surface somewhere out of the way, and either deliver or receive something or other."

"What sort of 'something', though? Some sort of weapon, perhaps?"

"Possible, but it would have to be something out of the ordinary if Jerry thinks it will turn the tide of the war. He *must* have realised by now that he's running out of options."

"So, something small enough to be transported on a U-boat."

"And powerful enough to create major damage and injury."

"Quick and cheap to produce and distribute."

"A final solution?"

Ole Jerg's first contribution brought an instant, total silence over the group. Captain Peter Yates looked at the priest in curiosity.

"Why do you choose precisely *that* phrase, Ole?"

Ole looked embarrassed but cleared his throat and tried to express himself more succinctly. "Well, if Germany really is in such a critical mess as you all seem to think—and remember, we civvies don't get to hear even a tenth of what you obviously know and deal with on a day-to-day basis—then the *Führer* must be getting desperate, and he's likely to be looking for a dramatic gesture of some sort. Some new type of weapon, something which can have a knock-on effect, perhaps a *disease*...a biological final solution...so to speak." Ole faltered and floundered to a stop as he saw the expression in Peter Yates's eyes change to something less serious. Confused at the thought that he had unwittingly said something which his colleague found faintly amusing, he stared mutely, demanding an explanation without saying a word.

Eventually, Pete nodded. "Of course, there was no reason you could possibly have known, but all the same!" He looked for and received tacit permission from Jim and Johnny to continue acting as spokesman before continuing.

"The phrase 'The Final Solution' is one which our intelligence services discovered some time ago as a coded reference routinely used throughout the Nazi regime. They plan to promote their ideal of a pure Aryan race, a plan which includes executing every Jew living in Germany. Your choice of phrase was, to say the least, somewhat unexpected. Especially coming from one who is an ordained priest."

"What are the chances, though?" Ole protested. "I mean, first they'd have to develop the weapon itself..."

"Just remember, up until the mid-thirties, Germany could boast the world's best-equipped universities and research labs—and the scientists to man them," Peter Yates cautioned.

"They'd still have to find a way to use the weapon," Johnny argued.

"Without being affected themselves, Johnny? Trust you to bring up a practical point! But it's really a question of range when you come down to it. Long-range artillery shells or carpet-bombing a city—"

"That's all very well, Jim, but you still have to be able to go in yourself and take control, without the risk of being infected."

"That could be something as simple as, for example, a two- or three-day quarantine period after the attack before you send in your own troops. You could leave it longer,

I suppose, and the longer you leave it, the easier it should be to design a biological agent with a limited lifespan."

"You'd still have the problem of dealing with the infected bodies of the victims," Ole objected.

"And the health hazards of the decomposing flesh itself," Commander Yates added. "Though I'd guess that masks and sterile gloves would go a long way to protecting against cross-infections."

"But that still leaves the one practical question unanswered," mused Jim, "which is: could such a bio-weapon be produced—in secret—and distributed to airfields or artillery positions or wherever you'd opt to launch them from? And all this, without any intelligence services finding out what was going on? Surely you could never maintain that level of secrecy. It's impossible!"

"This is all well and good—" Johnny Walker had been quiet for a few minutes, but he hadn't been idle. "–but it's all theory. Do we have any reports, sightings, rumours even—*anything* which suggests any traffic of any sort in that sector of the North Sea? Because unless this U-boat has someone to meet..."

"Point taken, Johnny. It might be nothing at all. If we could just work out a possible reason for them undertaking the journey in the first place, I'd feel easier. I confess, the fug in here's starting to give me a headache. I need some fresh air."

Brigadier Nolan looked up at the wall clock.

"The last train's gone, but the pubs are still open for another hour or so. We can slip out the front door without anyone being any the wiser."

Once the security camera confirmed that the passage outside the door was not in use, they slipped out into the subdued lighting which was adopted during blackout hours and made their way to a family-run pub called Ye Cracke, a small hostelry off Dale Street which started to look overfull when the customer tally reached double figures. On the other hand, the landlord was Peter Yates's cousin, and for that reason, discretion was always guaranteed.

An hour later, Brigadier Nolan was regretful but resolute. "I said I needed the air, gents, and I'm certain you all did, too. But one pint's enough to be going on with, and we've a lot still to get through. We'd best leave *before* your cousin calls 'Time!' It'll attract less attention if we slip out now."

\* \* \*

WO2 Warren was ready to admit them through the sluice when they returned to the top of Water Street, and he'd used the time profitably to air the underground bunker of the build-up of tobacco smoke, collect coffee mugs and generally freshen up the room.

"Bill, you've been on duty all day." Peter Yates was suddenly struck with pangs of conscience.

"It's not a problem. I can bunk down in the dormitory, and be on hand."

Despite his protests, Bill was shooed out of the planning office.

Johnny Walker returned to the still shots of the U-boat, still pinned to the wall.

"If he was supposed to be *meeting* someone..." he muttered.

"Then why is there no trace of *any* other shipping in the area?" Brigadier Nolan completed the thought.

"But if he *isn't* there for a pre-arranged meeting, we're looking for a logical reason for him being there at all. There's no military or tactical advantage to be gained from it, for starters," growled Commander Yates.

"Now I know what's missing," Johnny Walker suddenly exclaimed.

"It's the second U-boat! Where'd *he* bugger off to? There's no record of him since they split to pass Fyn! Are there any reports of a U-boat being spotted, fired upon, maybe sunk?"

A rash of phone calls and telex messages followed, all without result.

"Can we be certain there were two U-boats to start with? How good is the source?"

"Perfect track record. Thoroughly dependable."

"Okay, let's think. Lille Bælt is quite narrow. Could he have had second thoughts and doubled back around to pass Fyn to the east, same as the first one?"

Johnny Walker thought for a moment, then nodded. "That's what I'd be inclined to do. I'm a bit surprised the commander even attempted to pass through Lille Bælt. Anyone who can read a chart would realise there's next to no chance of slipping through unobserved."

"Perhaps we should be looking further south, back towards Fyn and Sjælland. Unless we get proof to the contrary, we have to assume the two U-boats are on the same mission, travelling together."

"And all we have to decide is, why," commented James Nolan with a tired smile.

"What size crew is there on your typical U-boat, Johnny?" Peter Yates asked.

"Depends on the class, Sir. We know of mini-subs built for clandestine work—sabotage and the like—which can be crewed by two or three and have almost no free crawl space inside 'em! Then there's a range of vessels of varying sizes— if this is one of the most recent developments, they'll be the model we've called Class Seven. We reckon they have a crew of about fifty."

"Including the captain and officers?"

"Probably, but the fewer crew members you have to cater for, the more efficient you can be. Just recycling the air becomes a major logistical problem if you're spending most of your time underwater."

"So, fifty, possibly fifty-one including the captain. Fifty-two? Where do we draw the line?"

Johnny Walker sat back and appeared to treat Pete's question seriously. "The more crew there is in a U-boat, with a finite amount of breathable air, the more difficult it becomes to function efficiently. Personally, I'd go for the least possible—fifty—which allows for three eight-hour duty shifts of sixteen crew plus two senior officers. Fifty-one as an outside bet. Fifty-two, I'd say, is out of the question!"

"Why's that, Johnny? And don't think I haven't noticed that look in your eye. Out with it!"

Johnny Walker nodded his acknowledgement of being caught out, but delivered his punchline anyway. "We all know about Hitler's reputation for being highly superstitious. Quite simply, fifty-two is a multiple of thirteen, and I don't think he'd *allow* any ship to have a crew of fifty-two—or thirty-nine, or sixty-five or—"

"Okay, Johnny, we've got the picture."

Johnny's facetious but more than half-serious reasoning to justify his valued judgement was accepted at face value and eased the tension that had been building again.

A glance around the table resulted in mutual nods of agreement, and they decided to call it a night. As if responding to a signal which none of them had thought to send, WO2 Warren appeared at the door with a tray of hot drinks.

"Spot on!" murmured Commander Yates as he took the nearest mug of cocoa.

"This will certainly help us sleep!" added Johnny Walker, who was suddenly aware of the fact that it was twenty-four hours since he'd last seen a bed of any description, and that wasn't his own bed, either. "I don't care which bed I crash on. I can't walk any further!" With a groan, he sat on the nearest bed to the door and kicked off his shoes. Draining the scalding cocoa in his mug at a single gulp, he collapsed onto the narrow, metal-framed bed and was asleep almost before his head hit the pillow.

# Chapter Seven

Sometimes it was easier to give advice than it is to follow it. He'd had to rely on the depth reading from *U-534*'s gauges when he'd ordered his crew members to evacuate. He *knew*, with absolute certainty, that he was less than thirty metres from the surface, but his instincts all screamed at him to keep what he had in his lungs instead of exhaling to compensate for the decrease in pressure, which emergency protocols claimed was vital to avoid serious injury.

He forced himself to release a miserly amount of air. Immediately, he felt the pressure ease fractionally on his chest and in his ears as he sped towards the surface, clinging to the object he had discovered in the torpedo hatch he had been instructed to use in the event of an emergency evacuation. His speed was increasing as the pressure decreased: the tube he clung to so stubbornly fought as if it were a wild, unbroken mustang attempting to unseat him and make its bid for the freedom which beckoned so tantalisingly close. He just had to hang on for a few more seconds.

Suddenly, shockingly, incredibly, it was over. He felt the angle of ascent flatten out as he and his mount burst from the cold, unforgiving waters his lungs were not equipped to breathe and arced into the air before bellyflopping ungracefully back to float on the surface. His body convulsed: he coughed, choked, vomited, then discovered that he could breathe. Wonderful, fresh, life-giving air! He sucked it greedily into his tortured lungs and lay unmoving on the tube, which floated, dormant and docile, between his thighs.

Nollau was forced to allow whatever current there might be to dictate his direction of travel. He had no strength to fight it, and coming down from the adrenaline high he'd ridden during his unorthodox escape from the stricken U-boat left him feeling totally spent, both physically and emotionally. After a few minutes, he'd recovered sufficiently to force himself into an approximately upright position and take stock of his surroundings.

There were no vessels to be seen, but from such a low vantage point, that didn't mean a great deal. His horizon couldn't be more than five kilometres in any direction, but the open vista of a deceptively calm sector of the North Sea offered nothing his eye could focus upon to judge dimensions or distances.

He needed a point of reference, and as he coaxed his makeshift life raft around a few degrees, he was rewarded with the sight of land, which he judged to be within paddling distance. A further stroke of luck: what current there was seemed to be working in his favour. His heart pulsed stronger, the blood coursing more swiftly through his veins, flooding his entire body with renewed energy. As he lined up the improvised escape float, he felt the lightest of breezes across his shoulders: it seemed he was going to get another touch of fortune. He was going to need all the luck he could get if he were to reach the relative safety of dry land. For the moment, whatever was contained within the tube upon which he floated was not important. The only thing that mattered was his survival.

He forced himself to establish a rhythm, breathing deeply as he lay once more on his stomach and began a splay-armed version of front crawl strokes either side of the mysterious cylindrical object, the one thing separating him from an ignominious death by drowning. From time to time, he glanced up to check his overall progress and make sure he hadn't wandered too far off course. It appeared that the wind and the current were holding. The island loomed straight ahead, and before long, he could see that he was considerably closer than he had been: so close, in fact, that he couldn't miss it.

The water became appreciably warmer and paler, which told him he was now in the shallows and reminded him that, according to the emergency protocols he'd studied on the way to becoming a naval officer, the greatest danger for shipwrecked sailors was hypothermia. At the first opportunity, he'd have to strip out of his sodden uniform and either dry it or—preferably—steal some civilian clothing in its place. Wherever he'd finished up, it most certainly wasn't Germany or German-occupied territory, and his uniform would be a distinct handicap if he were to have any chance of completing his assigned task.

As he splashed along, making slow but steady progress, he had time to study the object which had already saved his life at least once by carrying him safely away from his first command ship; twice, if he took its usefulness as a buoyancy aid into the equation, which he was quite happy to do.

It was surprisingly light for its size, and very buoyant: this led him to guess that it was not constructed of metal or any other heavy, durable material. He had assumed it to be some sort of top-secret weapon but couldn't think of any weapon effective in modern warfare that would not be constructed of durable, metal parts. And why so much protective padding? If it was that delicate, he couldn't imagine it being of a great deal of use as a weapon, and he didn't think all the careful packaging was entirely to protect it from prying eyes, either.

For the moment, all that mattered was that it floated, it appeared watertight, and he was not in any immediate danger of drowning. For this, he supposed, he should be grateful.

Suddenly, he was forced to put his speculations to one side as a wave, which was significantly stronger than anything so far, slapped against the leading edge of his one-man escape raft, showering across his face. He sat up at once and discovered that he was less than fifty metres from a deserted, empty beach. The water was not much paler in colour, but he could feel the soles of his shoes graze along some sort of solid ground: stone, pebble, sand, it made no difference. The water was now so shallow he could stand, dismount and push or pull his ride up onto the beach.

He'd been riding so long, the muscles in his legs were stiff and painful, and the pins and needles in his toes and the soles of his feet were further confirmation of prolonged lack of use. Standing beside his primitive canoe, the water reached almost to his hips; he braced and forged ahead, pushing the rescue craft with his right hand, until his knees were exposed. He paused, bent down and tried an experimental heft: the object was indeed as light as its extreme buoyancy had suggested, and he was able to balance it across his shoulders. With the last of his remaining strength, Nollau carried it the last few metres onto the warm, dry sandy foreshore, dragging it beyond the highest point the tide had reached recently before collapsing into some low but dense undergrowth. He hoped it would conceal both himself and the package he had been charged to deliver long enough for him to recover his strength and continue to serve the Reich as best he could.

He felt himself on the point of total collapse, but the combination of good officer training and even better self-discipline reminded him of his earlier thoughts on the danger of hypothermia. The day was pleasantly warm. As he quickly stripped off all his clothing, he decided it was not yet mid-morning, and it looked as if the weather would remain warm and dry. By the time he had draped his uniform on the closest bushes, his body was screaming for rest. He barely had time to crawl deeper into the undergrowth and lie flat on his back, using the watertight, sealed package as a pillow, before he tumbled into a dreamless sleep of exhaustion.

When Nollau regained consciousness, the sun had travelled across the sky and sat close to the treeline, casting long shadows that lay across the bushes where he'd slept, cooling him just enough to rouse him.

The one thing he hadn't taken off was the top-of-the-range Swiss chronometer his father had presented to him when he passed his exams and became a naval officer. He studied it, hoping it had survived both shipwreck and waterlogging: it continued to tick discreetly, and there was no evidence of jerky, irregular movement in the sweep of the second hand as he watched it complete a full circle. He had to assume that it still functioned, and that the time it showed was correct. Six o'clock, all but a minute or two: from the sun's position, that had to be evening, not early morning. Two discreet windows inlaid in the face of the watch confirmed that the date was Friday, 4th May.

Nollau took a moment to offer thanks to his father for the watch, which at least told him something about the *when* of his current situation: now all he had to do was discover exactly *where* he'd finished up.

However, it was a question of first things first. Such matters included collecting all his clothing, which he sincerely hoped would be dry by now, and getting dressed. After that, he had to find somewhere safe to spend the night. Most likely, he'd go to bed hungry this first night, but drinking water was also a priority.

His boots were the one item not completely dry, but he hadn't planned on walking any further than absolutely necessary in this as yet unknown, anonymous island. All he could be certain of was, it was a long way inside enemy territory: he suspected it was one of the many islands dotted around the Kattegat and therefore nominally Danish territory.

It was as good a time as any for an equipment check: Nollau needed to know what he had on hand before he decided what his next steps should be. One thing was sure: whatever might be happening in the world outside his present location, he had been entrusted with the delivery of an item, something which was supposedly vital to the war efforts, something so powerful it would turn what seemed to be a lost cause into a resounding victory for the Fatherland. He had no clear directions regarding who he should deliver it to, nor any instructions as to where the handover was supposed to take place. He decided that, as an absolute minimum, he had a right to know what it was he had promised to deliver.

He glanced again at the sun. This far north, and in May, there was at the very least an hour, maybe an hour and a half of good daylight to work with.

Amongst the items he had taken from his pockets and stacked neatly on a flat stone before spreading the uniform to dry was a standard-issue folding blade knife and multi-tool. He'd never needed to use it until now and breathed a silent prayer that the blade was sharp enough and strong enough for his intended purpose.

He wriggled the package out from under the shrubs and laid it across the top of three or four bushes which grew close together and formed a reasonably level work surface at thigh height. In handling it, he was once again struck by the lightness of the whole package, even allowing for the copious amounts of protective covering.

The first layer was some sort of clear plastic, but it wasn't an everyday, easily ripped thin membrane. This plastic consisted entirely of small, evenly sized, air-filled bubbles.

Its purpose was most likely to shield whatever was inside the package from shock and bumping about. As he worked from one end, he discovered that there were several overlapping layers of this bubble-wrapping and concluded that it was also an excellent waterproofing, though whether that had been part of its intended purpose was something he was in no position to pass judgement upon.

A few inches in from either end of the object, and close to the centre, three rings fitted snugly around the packaging. Similar to white collars, they were of a material he had never come across before. He tested it with his fingers: it felt brittle, snapped off easily, and resembled a cross between paper and card. Like the plastic, it had a bubble-like consistency. Nollau felt he ought to recognise it: he was sure he'd seen something similar once before…

That was it! It was similar to the buoyancy aids he had seen used in teaching children—and some navy cadets—how to swim. The detective in him reasoned that they served the same purpose in this application. He only needed to use minimal pressure to snap each of them cleanly in half and reach the next level of packaging.

Thin laths of balsa wood or some very similar material— he wasn't an expert carpenter—ran the full length of the pack, forming an open-weave frame which tapered to a point, held in tension by coiled wire: half a dozen neat turns or more at each end, and a single loop of wire equidistantly spaced throughout the roughly twelve-foot length of the object. Nollau was glad he had the other tool blades on his knife. Using the can-piercing tool and the screwdriver blade was far more effective than blunting the edge of his knife blade. Working methodically, and without haste, he soon had the wooden frame parted without damaging any of the parts. He was careful to stack everything he dismantled in separate piles. They were, after all, a resource of sorts, although at the moment he had no clear idea how he might be able to use them.

The final layer was a cloth of some sort. Not linen, nor was it wool or cotton. His experience with fabrics was very rudimentary, but it seemed to be waxy or oiled, offering further protection against the elements, he thought, but what was it protecting?

Slowly, and with great care, he unrolled it from one end. A smooth, pale wooden shaft began to appear. It was tightly grained, with long, straight lines no thicker than a human hair running evenly along its full length. In the low angle of the setting sun, they appeared to glow blood-red against the skin colour of the wood. It had a distinctive sheen, suggesting it had been polished and cared for, and that it was of considerable age. It was unlike any wood he had ever come across in his life.

There was one more surprise awaiting him, something he discovered as he unrolled the final foot of cloth from the top end of the object, which tapered as he approached it.

The tip of the object was metal, a blade with razor-sharp edges. It flashed in the red glow of the sun, and there were symbols, possibly letters, but not a language or even an alphabet he recognised. He rolled the last few loops of the bandage neatly, placed it to one side and picked up the tool.

Herbert Nollau stood in the dying light of the day, feeling in his fingertips the power throbbing through this secret weapon, the answer to his country's needs.

An ancient throwing spear.

# Chapter Eight

WHEN the glow from the tip of the spear started to lose its intensity, Nollau roused himself from the maelstrom of conflicting emotions which chased each other through his conscious and subconscious thought processes. He glanced at his watch, surprised to discover that the luminous digits were clearly visible. There was almost no light left in the day, and he appeared to have lost at least half an hour since his previous time check: had he been half-dozing while standing there, fascinated by the beauty of the artefact he had discovered buried beneath layer upon layer of protective coverings?

Certainly, that seemed to be the case. One thing had been decided for him, however. There was no question of even attempting to find somewhere else to sleep tonight. All the various elements of packing materials he hoped to recycle and reuse were close at hand, most of them just about visible. Quickly and efficiently, he gathered together everything large enough to suggest itself as a slightly more intense shadowy lump against the paler background of the sand dunes. He hesitated when he came to consider what he ought to do with the spear. He was strangely reluctant to put it down, or even release it from his grip, but holding it tightly through the night while trying to sleep seemed impractical.

He decided to lay the strips of balsa together, overlapping them slightly, and placed the spear on the improvised mattress. Taking the rolled-up cloth, he placed it close to the metal tip and laid his head on it, wrapping his arms and legs around its length as if sharing body heat with a living partner, wife or girlfriend. *Would our forebears have thought of a spear as having a 'female' nature,* he wondered to himself just before sleep claimed him. *We refer to 'the Fatherland', and navy personnel always think of ships as 'she'. Is there a consensus of opinion regarding the sexual identity of weapons?* He was sleeping soundly before his exhausted brain could form even the semblance of an answer.

# Chapter Nine

NOLLAU woke easily and without alarm, damp from early morning dewfall and slightly stiff, but a few minutes' vigorous exercise fixed both problems.

Nothing to eat, and no drinkable water: breakfast wasn't going to delay his departure. All he had to do before he left this unnamed beach was to make an inventory of what he had on hand and decide what he might possibly have a use for and what he needed to jettison. The one item he had to take with him was the spear itself. He took it in his hands and wondered if he should carry it openly to keep his burden as light as possible or rewrap it both to protect it from the elements and to avoid causing undue interest. One thing he knew: toting an ancient hunting spear in plain view was a sure way of attracting the attention of everyone he met.

The sensible thing would be to wrap it again; he knew this was the only logical thing to do but once again found he did not wish to release his hold on its smooth, polished bole. It seemed to throb with power when he held it, a power that somehow felt as if it were flowing into his body, energising and invigorating him. When he did, eventually and reluctantly, lay the spear aside to pick up the roll of wax cloth, it felt like a painful, physical loss.

He worked quickly to cover the spear's length, ensuring no part of it was exposed, and was relieved to discover that once he had repacked it, the innate throb of power and his desire to caress its surface were both reduced to tolerable levels. He secured the tightly wound cloth with a few of the loops of wire he'd set aside and sat back to take stock of the few possessions he had salvaged.

From his trouser pockets: apart from the folding knife, which he'd already found extremely useful, he had a few coins and a badly stained wallet containing a wadded mass of wet and almost valueless Deutschmarks, which he would not be able to use anywhere in Denmark. The best thing he could do with them, he decided, was to attempt to dry them out, separate them and use them to start a fire. He'd have to live off the land, catching and cooking his own food. He wasn't too concerned about that: his officer training had included intense periods of exercises intended to develop such survival skills, and as a young boy, he'd also been active in the local *Pfadfinderinnenverbände,* learning the simple lessons Robert Baden-Powell had sketched out when he established the fledgling Boy Scout movement in Great Britain.

There was only one item he would have wished for which he didn't currently possess. As a non-smoker, Nollau hadn't been in the habit of carrying either a lighter or matches. He knew that he could, at least in theory, use the magnifying effect of the slight bevel on the glass of his watch to concentrate the rays of the sun to start a fire: he had to hope it was as easy in practice. The sooner he could barter for or steal certain basic necessities, including a box of matches, the easier he would feel.

The laths of wood were too cumbersome, and he couldn't imagine them being of any use. On the other hand, they had to be buried: there was no point advertising his presence by leaving evidence lying around. The same argument held for the odd white not-quite-paper collars. Everything he wasn't going to carry with him had to be buried, which meant he could find a use for the wooden strips of balsa as makeshift spades to dig in the soft, easily worked sand of the foreshore.

His uniform was still reasonably presentable, but he couldn't be seen wearing it in public, behind enemy lines, even if 'little Denmark' was officially under the protection of the German Occupying Forces. He would have to make finding a civilian alternative his top priority, but for the moment, he could take consolation from the thought that he had plenty of pockets in both shirt and trousers to store the things he had decided were worth the trouble of keeping. This included the still-damp Deutschmarks, the remainder of the wire, his knife and a few short lengths of string. Many U-boat commanders habitually wore a fully functional sidearm as a part of their uniform. Herbert Nollau was not one of them: now he wondered briefly if his personal feelings of being uncomfortable around guns might put him at a further disadvantage. While it was true that he couldn't expect to be able to use any gun to blaze himself a path from his present location to the German border who-knew-how-many kilometres to the south, just a few rounds—a single full magazine—would have given him a much-needed boost of confidence. Still, what couldn't be cured…

At least he'd be travelling light. He looked around the immediate vicinity to check there were no signs of his bivouac he'd overlooked or forgotten to obliterate. As far as he could see, he'd covered his tracks, at least to any casual inspection. He glanced at his watch: six-thirty, and the lowest rim of the sun was just about to pull clear of the sparkling, empty waters of the North Sea. He turned his back to it and started to trek east, inland and slightly uphill. Assuming that someone actually lived on this island, they were most likely to be living along the coastline where they could catch fish for the pot, but his first concern was to get an overall impression of the lie of the land.

There didn't seem to be any trodden paths of any sort, but the first few hundred metres were open scrubland with no thick, impenetrable masses of bushes or trees to hinder his progress; nor did he come across any hand-built walls, fences or other signs of human endeavour. He was still climbing away from sea level: quite possibly, anyone building a permanent structure on the island would choose to do so inland, as a precaution against winter storms.

He paused and looked all around once more. To the east, back the way he'd come, he could still glimpse the sea. North, west and south seemed much the same: open grassland, apparently unworked, with no evidence of human habitation. Unconsciously, he hefted the spear in his hand, taking a more comfortable grip as he pondered his next move.

Even through the concealing cloth, he felt the spear warming against his palm. This time, the surge of power was stronger, more urgent. The spear was suddenly alive in his hands, tugging like a powerful dog kept on a brutally short leash: it demanded he turn to his left, southwards. The barely restrained energy could not be denied: it demanded to be borne in one specific direction. Nollau discovered he had no choice in the matter but to comply.

Nollau was acutely conscious of everything around him: he seemed to be experiencing every nuance of colour, the vaguest scent, as if for the very first time in his life. There could be no question about it, this could only be a direct consequence of handling the spear.

His vision blurred, and for a moment, he felt dizzy and thought he was about to faint. When his head cleared again, he found he was close to a small stand of trees which he was convinced had been some distance off to his left. Also, and without conscious memory of how it might have happened, he discovered that he had peeled the covering from the spear: the weapon now glistened, lacquered and perfectly balanced across his right palm. He could feel the covering, rolled into a neat ball and crammed tightly in his trouser pocket.

The muscles in his shoulder and arm tensed, and he watched as the spear arrowed at a precise spot, a clump of long grass about five metres away, near a bush no different to any other in the vicinity. A moment later, the handle juddered as the blade hit the ground and bit deep enough to remain standing at a forty-five-degree angle.

He had not thought of using the spear. For a start, it wasn't a weapon anyone living in the mid-twentieth century could have claimed to use. Furthermore, he hadn't consciously reacted to any hint of a target to aim at: the decision appeared to have come from the spear itself, as if it were a sentient object, endowed with independent life.

Nollau felt naked and defenceless without the weapon secure in his hand and hurried forwards to retrieve it. He knew in some mysterious fashion that there must have been a target, even though he hadn't seen it at the time. His theory was confirmed when he parted the grasses and discovered the spear's blade had passed through the neck of a plump rabbit, pinning it to the ground. His immediate thought was one of gratitude that the innocent animal had not suffered but had died instantly.

Here was the answer to one of his most urgent needs: provided he could coax life into a small fire, the rabbit would afford him at least one meal. Of course, he still needed water, and his combined first aid/survival lessons all agreed that this was more important than food.

The spear pulled easily from the sandy soil. As he gently removed the limp, still-warm body from the blade, a tiny shower of darkened granules of mixed blood and soil drizzled from the tip, bouncing off the back of his hand and sleeve cuff before scattering on the ground. Nollau examined the blade closely. It was pristine, without a trace of blood or earth clinging to it, something he would have thought impossible without the evidence of his own eyes. He shook his head slowly: there were too many things happening, far too rapidly, and all connected in some way with the spear. He raised it in thanks towards the rising sun, then brought it smartly back to the perpendicular and planted the heel of the weapon in the soil, close to his feet.

As the butt landed, Nollau was aware of the thousand and one tiny sounds of nature living and breathing all around him, noises which are normally ignored, overlooked because they are always there, a constantly changing, barely audible background to everything else. The gentle breeze whispered to him, carrying a treble descant melody from an unseen bird. The surf lapping the shore provided a rumble of *basso continuo*, and he also identified the welcome tinkle of running water somewhere close by. He concentrated on the sound and decided it was off to the right, towards two o'clock relative to his present position.

Letting his newly enhanced hearing guide him, he soon came across a small stream chattering over a pebbly base. Kneeling, he scooped a palmful of water to taste: cold and refreshing, with no bitter aftertaste of contamination, it was as welcome as the finest wine. He laid the spear to one side, settled close to the spring, and slaked his thirst. He was in no danger of dehydration yet, but it had been a long time since his last opportunity.

He was careful, however, not to overindulge: some half-remembered advice he'd read somewhere or heard in the course of a survival lecture suggested this was not a good idea. Squatting back on his heels, he looked around and made a decision. This was a good place to build a fire and experiment with the most practical way to cook a rabbit without a pan. First, though, he'd have to decide which parts of the rabbit he was going to cook. He tried to think if he'd ever seen the animal in any sort of 'ready to cook' state on a butcher's slab: sadly, he had to admit he'd never paid much attention to such insignificant details during enforced dutiful trips to the market at his mother's side.

Logically, however, at the very least he'd have to remove its guts, intestines and the like, as he couldn't imagine anyone wanting to cook anything other than the solid flesh. The same applied to the head and brains, though these were almost completely severed from the torso by the way the spear had sliced through the neck. That left the fur, which he had already worked out would have to be removed: it was sure to create lots of smoke, potentially advertising his unauthorised presence and leading to discovery.

When he began the dressing of his first meal using his pocket knife, he discovered to his dismay that the blade was already losing its edge. With a degree of reluctance, almost ashamed to use it for such a menial task, he turned to the spear as the only other cutting tool he had to work with.

It seemed he had but to touch the tip of the spear's blade against the carcass in order to make precisely the desired cut of exactly the correct depth and distance each time he laid his inexpert hand on the rabbit's body. Once he made the initial cut from throat to navel, he saw that a flap of skin had worked itself free from the edge where the spear had sliced the neck. The lightest of tugs eased the fur further from the rabbit's throat, and as he got a better grip on it, he discovered that skinning the animal was not as daunting a task as he'd thought it might be. By selective use spear's tip when he ran into difficulties, it took Nollau less than ten minutes to disembowel and skin his meal.

He glanced at his watch, then looked up at the position of the sun. Ten-thirty, and he could already feel the heat of the summer sun. The day could only get warmer, and there was no indication of any rain to come. He'd better experiment with his fire next. There was no point in constructing a makeshift rotisserie or spit to hang the meat on without first making sure he had something to hang it over.

In preparation, he gathered together every scrap of paper he'd managed to salvage, mostly the Deutschmarks, which he had a feeling would not burn too easily, though they were by now much drier than they had been the previous night. But then, reminded himself, everything was indeed, relative, as proved by the brilliant true-German scientist Max Planck ten years *before* the traitor Einstein published his inferior work and ran off to hide in America.

He stopped himself right there. Reliving the ranting nature of some of the lectures he'd been obliged to sit through at university was not going to help him survive, much less escape and complete the mission entrusted to him and his now-scattered crew. He took a few deep breaths to regain control of his emotions. When he was ready, he stretched out each sheet of paper, no matter how small, and secured it in place with a stone. By the time he had gathered some wood and sorted it, hopefully, they would all be dry enough to use as kindling. The spear lay with its point embedded in the sand, pinning the raw ingredients of his meal. The question of who he ought to deliver it to, or how, could wait until he had some idea of precisely where he was.

He strode to the top of the nearest sand dune, which gave him a reasonably unobstructed view of the island, for what he estimated to be at least a kilometre in every direction. There were no signs of any human endeavour: no crop fields, no buildings, obvious paths or roads, but he thought he could make out distant wisps of what may have been smoke but equally could have been steam rising from the newly warmed land. Descending the other side of the dune, he wandered along the edge of the beach, collecting wisps of dried grass and small twigs: with a limited amount of paper to start the fire, he needed any small kindling he could scavenge from nature's bounty.

Returning to the spring, he placed the kindling he had found alongside a smooth, flat piece of natural slate which he thought would be suitable as a firebase. With a miserly number of torn strips of paper and a similar amount of straw-bleached grass, he built the tiniest of tepees around the kindling with the smallest twigs he had.

Scarcely daring to breathe, he took the tip of his knife and pried the glass lens away from the face of his watch, praying that he wouldn't let sand in to gum up the works: it might not be essential to survival, but not having a sense of the passage of time would make him feel handicapped.

Removing the glass without accident or incident felt like a minor miracle in itself and gave him the confidence to continue: first, as a precaution, he wrapped his denuded watch inside a handkerchief.

He knew he had to hold the glass a certain distance from the dry tinder so that it could concentrate the strength of the sun's rays, but how to find the right distance? He tried a few experimental passes over the back of his hand, until he realised that the ideal distance was when a sun spot developed.

Holding the lens steady was a bit more difficult than he'd anticipated, but he persisted: in reality, he had little choice. Consciously, he caught himself *willing* the wisps of smoke to become more promising, the ember to develop, to spark and result in a quivering, fragile suggestion of a tiny flame.

When the mini-miracle occurred, it was all over so quickly Nollau barely had the chance to react. Smoke became ember and straight to flame, causing him to lay the glass quickly to one side and begin patiently feeding small twigs to the growing flames. Soon he was able to add heavier, longer-lasting pieces of wood, and he knew he could relax: the fire wasn't going to die on him, after all. *Score one for the city kid!* he thought and turned his attention to the meat.

As he raised the spear, the impaled rabbit simply slid off, crumpling to the ground. Nollau thought this curious. He had made no attempt to remove the spear: the blood should have congealed, making it more difficult.

Even more curious: there wasn't a trace or suggestion of blood on the spear, not even on the metal tip which had been *inside* the meat for several minutes. As he stood with it in his hand, he saw a cascade of grains shake themselves free, as if repelled from the spear by somehow taking on an electrical charge. Again, he felt a tremor, a thrill of power that shuddered from the spear, causing the muscles of his right arm to contract and forcing him to grip the handle more securely.

He was bemused, mesmerised almost; however, there were more pressing things to attend to. The flames of his intended cooking fire were now healthy but ravenously hungry, demanding more fuel. Quickly, he placed several sturdy logs over and around the central embers.

With the fire ready, Nollau considered how best to cook the rabbit. Should he try ramming it onto a fairly straight stick as a form of primitive spit, or should he try to find some mud and water, attempt to bake it in a primitive clay oven? He was reluctant to leave the campfire and opted therefore to take the first option, the spit. There was a long, slender branch with no leaves on it standing at right angles to the trunk of a nearby tree. Sawing it off with his knife, he inspected the cut ends and decided that the branch was still sufficiently green that it could be hung over the flames without great risk of it catching fire. As long as he had a decent supply of wood close at hand, he could squat and rotate the stick until he was satisfied his meal was ready. He fashioned two stands from four shorter lengths of stick, secured them with the pieces of string, and stuck them into the sand on either side of the fire.

"Neck end or arse end?" He stood with the remaining length of stick in one hand and the rabbit in the other, debating which was the best point of entry. Then, realising it didn't matter, pushed the stick through the rabbit, front to back, and propped the ends of the makeshift spit in the stand.

Given his hunger, the cooking process was less hasty than he'd have liked, but eventually, there were no pink bits and hardly anything overdone or charred, apart from the odd tufts of fur, which didn't count. While he ate he considered his options: stay one more night or move on and keep moving? He didn't think there was any real urgency forcing him to keep moving: he was certain nobody had seen him coming ashore, or they would have arrived by now. He could afford the time to explore a little, which might also have a bearing on his decision to stay or go.

# Chapter Ten

Nollau buried the remains of the food and banked the fire: there was no point in letting a perfectly good fire go out, one which he'd already put lots of work into. He strolled over towards the low-hanging tree at the edge of the sandbanks. The boots: they were going to be his main problem, as they were still wet, and he couldn't hope to get very far unless he could wear them or steal a replacement pair.

Rather than do nothing, which was clearly wasting hours of daylight he could be putting to much better purpose, he decided to explore a little further barefoot. His first brief recce, he recalled, had not revealed any evidence of paths or tracks close at hand: as long as he kept his eyes open for sharp objects underfoot, he thought he could manage. Being barefoot—at least, in theory—would also give him the advantage of being able to move stealthily and silently if a situation arose that required him to remain undetected.

A final check assured him that the fire had sufficient fuel on it to last for a while, and that the fuel was not going to push large, visible clouds of smoke into the sky, revealing his location.

He decided to start circling clockwise from his start position, taking that as six o'clock on a standard clock face. He crouched low and slowly, methodically, made his way from one bush to another until he reached as close as he could judge to where twelve o'clock would be. Faint murmurings of nature—birdsong and similar—were all he could identify: he didn't know whether this should please him or not, for the moment. He supposed evidence of human habitation would increase his chances of getting *off* the island, but that had to be put in perspective: on a deserted island, he wasn't going to end up a PoW.

From there, he circled a further semicircle, this time counterclockwise, ending about fifty yards or so from his start point. Still no evidence of footpaths, animal tracks, litter or other signs of a human presence. He squinted against the sun and identified the shimmer of air above his fire, perhaps a hundred yards away. He was on a slight rise, not quite enough to be dignified as a knoll or sand dune but enough to be called a vantage point.

He faced east and tracked to his right, following the curve of the beach he'd landed on until it blurred into the blue of open sea. Remaining rock still, he followed the beach in the opposite direction, and was gratified to confirm that yes, he *was* on an island, not the mainland. A small victory, perhaps, but it proved he was capable of logical thought: with few tools or material possessions, he had to be grateful for every little thing that might work in his favour.

Well, there certainly wasn't another landmass east of his current location, whatever this particular outcrop of rock was called—assuming it was big enough to *have* a name. He could recall the main islands in the Kattegat: the last one they had passed had been Anholt, scene of a minor skirmish early in the current conflict in which a German frigate had taken the island single-handedly. He could also recall a rough triangle of a shape to the northeast of Anholt but hadn't really taken a lot of notice because he didn't have orders to make it a point of reference.

Try as he might, the name stubbornly refused to come, but he thought the island was at least as big as Anholt, and therefore there was a better than even chance that someone lived there. He was almost certainly going to be forced to become a 'picker-up of unconsidered trifles' on his way to rejoining the civilised world. His uniform, for example, made him a marked man as soon as he met any adult. And as for how to carry the spear with him, that was a question for which he had no answer whatsoever. One thing was certain, though: he had been given clear orders to deliver the object to someone else—someone far higher than himself in the pecking order. He might not have been given a name, but that was irrelevant. He was honour bound to deliver the spear to a higher-ranking German officer, and that must now become his sole objective. Leaving it here on the beach of this still-unidentified Danish island was *not* an option. Wherever he went, the spear would go with him.

\* \* \*

The day was sifting away between his fingers: although his watch, if it still worked, was back with his boots, he could see the sun was approaching its midday zenith—which had to be south of where he stood.

There was only one direction he could explore, and that had to be due west, keeping as straight a line as he could—as long as his boots were dry enough to wear. The last thing he needed was blisters on his feet.

Returning to 'base', he unwrapped his watch and with all the care and precision of a professional jeweller replaced the glass. It continued to tick, which was encouraging, and he was reasonably sure that no sand had managed to lodge in the mechanism.

The boots had lost some of their mirror-polished sheen but none of their suppleness, as far as he could tell. He thanked his stars that he had been careful to set an example for his crew by keeping his footwear polished to impeccable standards day in, day out. More important was the fact that he couldn't feel a trace of dampness anywhere, not even right down inside the boot, around the toes.

He wouldn't be coming back to the spring: there was no further need for the fire, which was now nothing more than an indication to the next passer-by that someone had been there recently. Tossing the unused fuel into the bushes, he scuffed together dry sand from every side towards the central flat stone, scuffing over his footmarks as he did so. He stood back and surveyed the result: it wouldn't fool a skilled tracker, but at first glance, it wasn't too obvious.

Picking up the spear, he once again felt a surge of power, which worked on him like an instant caffeine jolt or an adrenaline rush. He'd been half-expecting it, considering what had happened on two previous occasions, and the anticipation was probably the only reason he didn't immediately drop the spear in surprise.

There was just one question he still had to find an answer for, and that was: how should he be carrying it? At three metres, it was designed for use as a throwing weapon and was easy to carry in one hand, but that felt wrong, somehow. It wasn't as if he was going to use it as a weapon if he were unfortunate enough to meet someone on his travels, though whoever he met would almost certainly have hostile intentions towards anyone wearing a German uniform, but carrying it at port—ready to use—didn't seem appropriate.

Sloping it formally over his shoulder, parade-ground style, didn't appeal, either. He tried to conjure a picture of himself doing just that along a country lane: the image was too childishly stupid for him to even contemplate. Quite apart from being a touch too long to be comfortable, the possibility of carrying it the way a rambler—or a shepherd?—might carry a staff seemed disrespectful. *Disrespectful of what?* he had to ask himself. *Of the spear*, was the immediate and unequivocal answer. This conviction was suddenly rooted in his brain, so swiftly that he simply knew it was an incontrovertible fact. The spear was from a bygone era—epoch might be a more precise term—and had already influenced him to the extent that he was in no doubt that it had earned *and deserved* respect.

The only remaining alternative seemed to be for him to carry it at what he supposed might be called half-port, with the butt in his right hand and his left hand half-open close to the tip, supporting it in front of his body at an angle of about forty-five degrees. The posture reminded him of his (very) young days as an altar server, carrying candles for special Masses on High Feast Days in his local church; how many years back *that* had been, he hardly dared think. Somehow, though, the reverence of the church ceremonies seemed a more appropriate way of acknowledging the respect that he was certain the artefact deserved.

\* \* \*

Having no trails to follow, Nollau lined himself up with the sun high and to his left. It was the only fixed point of reference he could use, until and unless he—literally—stumbled across something which had been placed on the map by human hands, such as a road sign, a building or a road of some sort.

The spear was no burden: he felt strength flowing from it directly into his body as he stepped carefully in a semi-crouch across the open meadows. All his senses were at full alert as he made for a line of trees where he would be less exposed to possible discovery.

It was cooler out of the sun, under the broad-leaved canopy of the natural woods. The only drawback, he realised, was getting turned around and wandering from his intended westerly direction, but he thought he could see enough of the sun's position to stay reasonably well orientated. There was quite a lot of deadfall and piles of leaves from the previous autumn, indicating this was not a managed woodland with regular ranger patrols and maintenance. On the one hand, it was impossible for him to move silently through this undergrowth; on the other, there were, as far as he could see, no grounds to fear discovery. Apart from natural sounds such as birdsong and a delicate breeze soughing in the upper branches, the woods were silent.

As the trees thinned and came to an end, he breathed a sigh of relief. Before him was a cultivated field, some sort of crop, which he, a streetwise city boy, didn't recognise in its natural, unpackaged state. He knew it couldn't be rice, not in Northern Europe: beyond that, it could have been anything from oats to potatoes.

Raising his gaze to the immediate horizon, he could make out thin plumes of smoke, indicating houses just out of sight. He hunkered down and thought for a moment. Was it worth taking a chance by crossing an open field, or should he start to think like a feral creature and take the long way around the perimeter in order to stay within the protective screen of the woodlands?

Better to err on the side of caution, he decided, and turned left to follow the edge of the woods leading him around the southern boundary of the planted area. He had to assume that the farmer would be checking on the crop's progress while the daylight lasted. He would be able to move more freely during hours of darkness, and if he was going to steal clothing, tools, even transport, then that was best left until night's blanket could keep his presence on this still-unnamed island secret from the rest of the world.

He took his time, pausing frequently to conserve energy. The handmade fencing that marked the end of the plot some brave soul had decided to plant turned roughly northwest, as far as he could judge it from the sun's position, and gave way to a mixture of marsh and fenland, which had obviously been considered not worth the effort of taming. Shadows were by now lengthening, and he decided that this would be a good place to rest. The warmth of the late-afternoon sun would make it easy for him to relax comfortably and sleep: he could keep himself warm during the cooler hours of the night by being active, on the move: and somehow he had to steal a boat if he was going to get off this island and complete his self-appointed mission to deliver the spear to a higher authority somewhere.

No point worrying about that just now: one thing at a time, he chided himself. His survival depended on keeping focused on the small, needy things of the moment. Time enough to worry about the bigger picture later.

He was still a solitary figure on the landscape, or so it seemed. In the middle distance, slightly to his right, he caught the flash of sunlight on open water. Assuming it was drinkable, that was a possible solution to his main concern. As a raw recruit on basic training, it had been hammered into him that the human body can endure far more from lack of food than deprivation of liquids: water was, therefore, more important to survival than food. From what he could see, there appeared to be a series of small lakes running roughly east to west. If he adjusted his course to keep them on his right, he could continue in the direction he wanted to travel without having to ford them, should they prove deep enough to hinder progress.

Gauging the distance to the presumed western shoreline of this plot of land wasn't easy, especially for someone who had never had to develop such skills, but it wasn't a particularly big island on the official maps of the area, certainly not big enough to have caught his attention when planning raids, and that meant it wasn't beyond the capabilities of any reasonably fit submariner to cross it: he didn't believe it could be more than ten kilometres wide, maximum. Satisfied, for the moment, he carefully laid the spear pointing in the direction he wished to continue after nightfall and composed himself to rest and sleep in the warm May sunshine.

When the breeze stiffened and changed direction to blow off the land and out to sea, Nollau woke naturally.

Roused by the drop in temperature rather than the increase in wind speed, he sat up and gazed around the scene. The sun still hung on the horizon, but not for much longer. It was time to move off, while he still had what advantage could be gleaned from the half hour or so afterglow of the sun's reflection in the clouds—something else which hadn't been a factor all day long. Clouds were forming rapidly, and while they might help retain the heat of the day, they also held a threat of rain.

Nollau was thankful he'd had the foresight to place the spear pointing exactly at his selected destination. He slipped easily into the semi-feral, crouched alert he'd unconsciously adopted earlier that afternoon and concentrated on where to place his feet, mindful of the uneven tussocks and occasional patches of bogland there to trap the unwary. The waterways were still just too far away to tell if they were natural or manmade: he thought they might possibly be the result of digging peat from the land for use as fuel.

As the shadows lengthened into full night, he found that an occasional glance ahead was sufficient to keep him on course. In what felt like a polite reminder, the spear tugged at his arm occasionally: was it possible that the weapon was imbued with some mystical power, guiding him on the safest, most direct route home?

The ground underfoot became damp but stopped short of turning boggy or treacherous. He could hear running water, and the sound reminded him of the long hours since he last drank. Just over a hundred paces from his chosen route across the fens, he was rewarded with the sight of the newly risen moon catching on a shallow stretch of running water. He stared hard, willing his eyes to confirm what he most needed to know: that it was running downhill and *away* from him. This had to mean...

He scooped a palmful and tested it: there was a slightly bitter back-taste but nothing unpleasant. More importantly, it was fresh, not salt.

Shirt off, he removed his watch and knelt on the bank to scoop cool, refreshing water over his head and shoulders before taking double handfuls of the life-saving liquid. When his thirst was quenched, he knotted his shirtsleeves around his shoulders and retraced his steps back to the firmer ground he'd been travelling before his pitstop. Loping parallel to the moon's silvery reflection in the stream, he moved more rapidly and with greater confidence, secure in the anonymity of the night, recharged by such a simple, basic commodity. He hadn't realised how close he'd been to a dangerous level of dehydration.

He made a conscious effort to up his pace, now he was covered by full dark. In a rural setting such as this, there was little enough reason for anyone to be abroad after dark during years of peace and plenty: during a time of war, the chances of anyone being abroad and wishing to challenge an unidentified shadow were close to nil.

He leapt with an almost feline grace from one tussock to the next, his feet finding each one unassisted by his eyes, which were more and more often concentrated on seeing ahead, surveying the bigger picture. There was a dim light, perhaps from a paraffin lamp or similar set to burn inside a small cottage a few hundred yards to his left, but he ignored it. He sensed he was close to his first objective: reaching the west coast of the island where, with any luck, he might be able to steal a small boat, even a change of clothes. From this side of the island, he was certain he would be able to catch a glimpse of the Danish mainland. Something clicked into place: he still hadn't worked out the name of the small island on which he'd been marooned for more than twenty-four hours, but now he remembered that the ferry between Denmark and Sweden left from a port not far from here, a large town called Frederikshavn. Something *that* size would surely be visible from this distance?

The ground he was walking upon began to take on a spongy texture, and he slowed, concentrating once more on where he placed his feet. The westbound stream had broadened out into a vaguely defined expanse of water, not exactly a lake but not worth calling a harbour or even an estuary. It resembled more marshland, and there was more evidence of human endeavour: small, ramshackle groups of young trees, saplings used as pilings, had been driven into the mud and shale, and planks and other pieces of scrap wood nailed to them as casual footholds here and there. They were not organised, nor did they appear to have an overall plan to them: they were, presumably, the results of the efforts of individual fishermen to have somewhere to moor their craft.

He didn't have to look too far. Just to the right of where he stood was a small boat, the open deck sheeted against the weather, and across the stern something he hadn't dared hope for: the squat, compact and unmistakable shape of an outboard engine. Now, as long as it didn't need an ignition key and it had a minimal amount of fuel in its tank, he could achieve his first goal: getting off this isolated island. The lights of the mainland seemed almost close enough to touch, but he was an experienced sailor and knew that distances, especially at night and in unfamiliar waters, could be deceptive. No need to get too excited yet, although the ripcord starter and full fuel can under the bench seat were promising.

Swiftly, Nollau laid the spear along the port side and in doing so discovered a serviceable pair of oars. He had worried about the risk of starting the motor to take his spoils of war out of the harbour, but now that problem had been solved. People living in isolated communities often sensed things others might not notice, but as long as he didn't have to contend with extremely strong currents, once he'd cleared mid-passage it wouldn't even matter too much if he didn't have enough fuel for the whole of the necessary journey. He could surely manage to complete the passage on willpower alone, as long as he had the oars to row with!

These thoughts and a dozen more fired across his mind haphazardly as he checked the vessel's seaworthiness and confirmed there were no signs of damage or leaks: every board seemed sound and dry. As a bonus, he found coffee, sugar and a small kettle, along with a plastic tank underneath the short seat in the prow of the vessel with a single word—VAND—painted on the side, next to a picture of a cup. He tested it: it was a bit stale-tasting, but definitely water, and the tank was more than half full.

There really wasn't anything else to hold him back: the moon slid briefly behind a cloud as he cast off the mooring ropes fore and aft and began a steady pull on the oars, keeping his eyes open for semi-submerged pilings and any debris until he made it out onto the unobstructed current of the narrow channel separating him from the mainland. The tug of the current tried to push him in a more northerly direction than he wished to go: shipping oars, he prayed for just one more undeserved slice of luck and pulled on the ripcord of the outboard motor.

His prayers were answered. The motor caught first time, and he quickly throttled back to run it at a minimum decibel level until he was well clear of the coast. After spending a day crossing the small island, speed was not his main consideration. All he had to do was ensure that his escape remained unnoticed, and to that purpose, stealth was more important to his mission right now.

# Chapter Eleven

JOHNNY Walker unbent from close scrutiny of the last few frames of film he'd been bent over for the last ten minutes or so, comparing frame-by-frame shots taken from the tail camera of Vixen Two. He had counted ten separate splashdowns, accounting for the depth charges unloaded as a safety precaution by the damaged Liberator in open sea where they could do no damage. The underwater explosions all tallied, sending up fountains of water in a fairly straight line and were more or less equidistant.

But there was something about the final drop that was different, somehow.

He rubbed his tired eyes and re-ran the last half dozen frames one more time.

"I'm getting segs on my eyes, Jim. Come and give me a second opinion here. There's something I can't quite…" His voice trailed off into uncertainty.

Brigadier Nolan wandered across the war room, ready to offer an opinion if he could. "Spotted something?"

"Maybe. Just have a look at the last couple of seconds of footage. I'm not certain, and I don't want to put ideas in your head, in case I'm imagining things…"

"I can hear a 'but' somewhere in there, Johnny. Unusual for you!"

"Just see what you think."

The 35 mm film ran across the spool, slowed to less than a quarter real-time speed. The final underwater detonation seemed to produce a markedly smaller geyser and ran into blankness as the light-sensitive film gave way to the runoff.

"Film's run out before the effects of the last—oh, hello! What was that?"

Stop and rewind: in the final few frames, a shadow appeared just after the water began to curl into a fountain.

"Where's that coming from? There's nothing recorded in the region. Have we disturbed a ditched plane or an earlier sinking?"

"It looks for all the world like oil or something similar." Jim was already reaching for the phone. "Records—any reports of action, sinkings or possible ditched planes for the following coordinates—immediate, this is urgent." He reeled off the coordinates printed on the edge of the photograph and replaced the receiver. "I want a recce plane over the area with a full reel of film. If there's a chance we've stirred up an old wreck, it could cause problems."

"And if it's something of more recent vintage, there's nothing of ours in the area," Peter Yates added.

"Nor on the surface," Johnny chipped in. "So that only leaves—"

"Your favourite target—a U-boat?"

Johnny nodded, his eyes gleaming with anticipation. "It's starting to look that way, and if it's damaged but still in one piece, that would be a *real* prize, well worth capturing!"

The phone shrilled once before Jim pounced on it.

"No records? You're sure? Thanks. Please patch me through to Middlesbrough. I want a plane up ten minutes ago with a full load of film, flight plan and target to follow once he's airborne and heading east. Have something scrambled while I work out the details."

\*\*\*

"Charlie Five to base. Approaching target, angels two north of Anholt, over."

"Charlie Five, go ahead."

"Flotsam and evidence of a strike below. Also dye, repeat, dye in the water."

Both sides regularly used dye to highlight life rafts and possible survivors of an attack. "Confirm, Charlie Five."

"Going in for a closer look, base."

"Understood, Charlie Five. Stay safe, don't get too close."

"Roger, base. Will remain out of range of hand weapons. Cameras running and set to record at range three to five hundred feet."

Turning on the proverbial sixpence, the Spitfire went into a steep dive, circling to flatten out at a heart-stopping 150 feet above sea level and slowing close to a stall speed to capture as much filmed detail as possible in a single pass.

"Base, I can see survivors in life rafts. They're about three miles north of Anholt. Any vessels in the region can divert? Over."

"Acknowledged, Charlie Five. Any signs of their vessel? Over."

"I'm heading due north. If there's any trace, that's where they appear to have come from. Stand by."

At low speeds, the Spitfire could become difficult to handle, but this was an experienced pilot, and as long as the film was still running he had every intention of recording as much detail as he could.

Tracking back, he found more evidence of a disabled vessel. Smaller pieces of flotsam bobbed sluggishly in oil-stained water, but there were no larger units of a surface ship. The last of the debris disappeared under his wingtip, a clean line cutting east to west suggesting that the survivors and the remains of their stricken vessel were all heading south on the prevailing current, towards the relative safety of Anholt as their nearest landfall. If they were the escaped crew of a U-boat, the vessel itself must have finished up in waters too deep to be probed with the basic radar installed on the Spitfire's instrument panel. Leaving his cameras running, the pilot banked one more time and headed for home.

*\*\*\**

"Looks like we hit something, Peter!"

"Credit where it's due, Johnny, if you hadn't spotted that tiny detail…"

"All the same, we've got a fix on the position, and—" Peter glanced at his watch "—with any luck, we've picked up the survivors by now, but they won't be processed or interrogated before tomorrow morning, earliest."

"What's the complement on these vessels again, Johnny? About fifty, did you say?"

"Correct, Jim. Possibly fifty-one, if the captain's not reckoned as crew."

"We'll just have to see if the whole crew escaped or are otherwise accounted for."

"Don't forget the British tradition of a captain going down with his ship. There's every reason to think the same applies in the German Navy. The sort of man who chooses to command a U-boat has to be a bit special, anyway!" Johnny commented. "Now, any chance of a few photos of the general area? I'm still not happy about a U-boat being this far from home, all alone, and especially when we've had reports of it being accompanied by another U-boat earlier in its voyage. Who were they trying to liaise with? Whoever it was didn't make the meeting, it would seem, so who was it supposed to be, and what happened to them? Christ, I hate unanswered questions, I really do!"

Johnny poured another coffee from the pot, oblivious to the fact that it was stone cold.

The teleprinter chattered a staccato message, catching them all unawares. None of them moved but stood and watched the message appear. In thirty seconds, it was over: the printer shuddered to a stop. There were three lines of text.

Jim Nolan looked around, accepted responsibility as senior officer present and strode across the room to detach the incoming message.

DTG 060652115z

Rescue of unconfirmed number of survivors by HMS frigate [redacted] from a position north of Anholt, Danish region of Kattegat. Oral reports suggest captain opted to remain with ship, other casualties possible.

APS Yarmouth

End DTG 060652116z

"Who or what is 'APS Yarmouth', someone?" growled Peter Yates.

"Jargon for 'All Possible Speed', Sir. It's common practice in most radio rooms, and abbreviations seem to help confuse Jerry if he's listening!"

"Hmmm." Peter seemed unimpressed with the explanation, but it was logical enough and didn't go against any security principles he could cite in critical response, so he let the matter lie. "We'll see if we can squeeze some gen out of the crew in the morning. They might be easier to crack if the captain's not there to scare the bejaysus out of 'em and keep 'em in line!"

"That's not likely to happen I'm afraid, Jim!" said Johnny Walker as he threw himself, exhausted, into the nearest chair. "The way Jerry works, everything's boxed off in isolated, watertight compartments, and that applies to the orders of the day, as well! I'll lay a penny to all Adolph's ill-gotten art treasures and Swiss bank accounts that the only person who knew the objective of this voyage was the captain himself. With him gone, we may never know who he was planning to meet."

"I suppose the only thing we can do is wait until the survivors have been interviewed, just in case the captain *did* manage to escape with them?"

"That'll take forever!"

"Do you have a better suggestion?"

"Have you—or has anyone—had any more bright ideas about the *purpose* of this voyage and all the secrecy and other precautions we already know about?"

This was almost the very first comment Ole Jerg had made since the military experts representing the British Army, Navy and Air Force had put their professional brains together. For over twenty-four hours, they'd torn up and redrawn various scenarios involving the eastern sectors of the North Sea without coming to any firm conclusions. Ole's role had been more that of water carrier, coffee maker and general calming influence. He'd sat in a corner, available if needed, and occasionally tidied away or collected mugs and washed them, keeping up an endless supply of the hot, strong, black-as-treacle coffee military brains seem to thrive upon. In quiet periods, he'd dug into his inner strengths and prayed sincerely for an outcome which would point to a justifiable and morally acceptable solution.

If someone had chosen that moment to drop the proverbial pin, it would have sounded as loud and brash as the opening bars of *Lili Bolero* leading into the latest news programme on the BBC. Peter, Jim and Johnny stared blankly at the unassuming representative of the clergy, confusion writ clearly on all three faces.

Johnny Walker was first to crack, but only by about half a heartbeat. "Ole, I'm sorry we haven't included you more in our disc!"

With a gracious and gentle wave of his hand, Ole managed to indicate that the apology was completely unnecessary. Somehow, he achieved this without needing to speak a single word.

"Gentlemen," he continued, "I've been present on many occasions when I've had to sit still and pray—often for periods much longer than this! Periods when a parishioner—or, more often, another member of the parishioner's family—has asked me to perform one or other of my official duties at the end of a long and eventful life.

"I knew when I was invited to join you that my role might be peripheral at best, perhaps to clarify a linguistic point and ensure that no terrible misunderstandings could occur. At the same time, I was brash enough to think that if I had the opportunity to sit quietly in a corner, my prayers for your guidance and success might have some value."

He looked from one to the next. There was no reproach, no judgement in his gaze: each of the senior officers present felt calmer, more relaxed, and more eager to hear what thoughts this humble man of the cloth might have to contribute.

"It was natural for you all, as men of action, to assume from the start that this U-boat—or these U-boats, plural, if we're going to be as accurate as possible—had a 'superweapon' on board." He laid the lightest of stresses on the one word he considered the most important in the sentence and paused before continuing. "But suppose there *isn't* some sort of superweapon involved?"

He looked at each again in turn, seeming to peer deep into each man's soul. "You admitted yourselves, any weapon being introduced into the conflict at this stage would take weeks to develop, months, probably, before it could be deployed and used, and we've all heard the most recent dispatches from each and every front where fighting is still taking place. Jerry's licked, he knows it, and he also knows he's run out of time! No, I don't think there's a weapon on board *U-534*. Not at all!"

"Go on, Ole!" Peter Yates murmured when the priest stopped once more, clearly embarrassed in front of such an attentive, if captive, audience.

"Suppose they had a passenger on board, or, looking at it from the opposite side, perhaps they were intending to meet someone? How important would that person's life have to be before it could significantly alter the length of the conflict, even have an influence on the actual outcome of the war?"

"It would *have* to be someone *very* special or important." Peter Yates seemed to be thinking aloud and unaware that he had voiced his thoughts.

"Well, it won't be Adolf nor his brother, Rudi, if the dockers at Cammell Laird have anything to say in the matter!" Johnny Walker's instinct in times of stress or danger was to stick two fingers up the nostrils of convention, and in particularly tense moments like this, he could generally be relied upon to ease the tension with an awful joke or more often an atrocious pun.

There was some truth to his flippant remark, however. Unconfirmed rumours had been flying around for some time, to the effect that Hitler's brother had succeeded in getting hired as a docker in Liverpool, but nothing was ever proved beyond all reasonable doubt. Traditionally, Liverpool dockers have never been known as students of the finer points of the law, and it had come as no surprise when a number of illegal immigrants working 'on the lump'—no insurance cards, cash in hand at the end of the day—disappeared. There were those who hinted that Rudi Schickenberger—Hitler's *real* family name—might have been one of them.

"I think we can agree with that, Johnny," James Nolan offered calmly. Nothing ever seemed to faze the cool, authoritative figure who was the public face of the RAF. "But rather than stating the obvious, such as, for example, a hundred and one different people it *couldn't possibly be*, it might be more useful for us to have a go at finding a name, or maybe a..." He snapped his fingers several times in frustration, seeking a specific word.

"A job, a role? A position in Government, perhaps?" This from Johnny again.

"Something like that, I suppose," James conceded. "Ole, you started this hare."

Ole looked blankly at him, as if he were talking a long-dead, obscure language.

"An old hunting expression, Padre. Hunting with hounds. The hare starts from wherever it's been hiding, and the dogs— not that I've ever *attended* a hunt. Horrible practice, blood sports! Anyway, I think you get the idea? Good! That's fine! Now, where were we... Oh, yes! Ole, you had a particular person in mind? Something you've heard about through the Church, perhaps?"

Was there just a touch more stress than absolutely necessary on the word 'church'? Ole took a breath and went straight in without preamble, not giving his colleagues a chance to dwell on the source of his information, as implied in the question.

"My job—my calling, the life I have chosen to live— means that I am frequently called upon to deal with people in appalling conditions, people who, through no fault of their own, have fallen upon bad times. I'm sure you'll appreciate that the same applies to *all* priests, of every denomination and variation of religion, irrespective of what title the minister, the gofer between Man and God, happens to choose or be given. Do we understand each other so far? Hmmm? Good!"

Ole seemed to be working himself up to a point which he at least regarded as being of vital importance.

"But there are certain things which I—as a priest forever, after the order of Melchizedek—hear, words spoken in the act of confessing that one has done wrong. These are words which no priest would *ever* repeat, and it's very, very important for me that you understand that before I'll say another word." He stopped, folded his arms, and looked around the table defiantly. "And I mean every word I've just said," he added, for good measure.

"We can accept that, Padre," said Peter Yates, glancing at Johnny Walker and James Nolan to make certain that he could act as spokesman for them as well and getting small but unequivocal nods.

"As long as you accept that there are extremely good reasons I cannot divulge my source this time...but it has come to my attention that at least *one* well-known and influential person is on the move, and he is due to arrive—" Ole paused and looked at his wristwatch. "—in less than three hours from now. Prince Haakon of Norway left the secure location in which he has spent his time in exile since Germany marched into his beloved country. He intends to rouse the people, to lead as a monarch ought to lead, from the forefront. He is determined that the Norwegian people, not just himself, should be *seen* to be actively taking steps to throw the Germans out of the country."

James Nolan whistled softly through tightly clenched teeth.

"I'm not going to ask you how you got this information, Padre, or from whom, but I can understand at least from whom, and under what circumstances, you could easily have been given this...this...well, what we call it doesn't really matter. It will never be repeated outside these four walls, anyway, and that's *another* expression you mustn't take literally, Ole. I'm well aware that this complex has more than four walls, but that's just part of the charm of the English language. 'Things are seldom what they seem', as one of the greatest poets of the last century once wrote.

"Now, can we get down to some practical business? I propose we send up a further recce plane, right now. I want an accurate fix on any vessel of any size which looks as if it might be heading for Norway, I want to know it gets there safely, and most of all, I want to know if there's *any* other traffic close by, which— No, forget that. Any other traffic, whether it seems interested in HRH's vessel or not!

"And let's not forget to sweep for things we can't see, as well. We know two U-boats left Lübeck, but we never actually *saw* either of 'em, just the wreckage from the one and presumed the other one had also been sunk with no survivors. There could well be a third one, and that could be the one *U-534* was supposed to link with."

# Chapter Twelve

The effort of plying a pair of oars in the slight swell of the waves as he pulled away from the makeshift jetty was enough to keep Herbert Nollau warm, and he was grateful. The air temperature had dropped rapidly when darkness fell over the Kattegat, and the muscles he was using were unaccustomed to prolonged exertion.

When he felt the gentle but persistent tug of the tide forcing him away off his chosen course, he shipped the oars and settled himself on the stern seat. He was heading for a point on the mainland somewhat south of the lights that he thought were Frederikshavn, the only town of any real size on this section of the Jylland coastline. Stripping the covers from the outboard motor, he hoped he hadn't shot himself in the foot by not checking it over before leaving. Yes, he'd made sure there was fuel in it and a spare can or two, but he had to trust it was mechanically sound.

The night was still and quiet, and as the dark, amorphous shape of the mainland coalesced and became a more solid shadow, he had time to think and formulate a plan of action. In truth, this was the first time since the moment he'd been forced to abandon his command he'd had time to think about anything which wasn't directly linked to a basic instinct to survive.

It seemed he'd chosen a time and place where he could make this first and most dangerous sea crossing in secret, unchallenged. He almost hoped that the German Navy was patrolling these waters, but perhaps that wasn't realistic, this far north and somewhat removed from the more frenetic, hotly contested arenas of conflict elsewhere in Europe—and Africa. *And Japan*, he had to remind himself. He sighed. This war, geographically, seemed to have sprawled out of anyone's control and grown to involve many more regions than any conflict which had gone before it. What did the *Führer* have in mind when he spoke of a 'glorious victory' and a *Reich* which would last for a thousand years?

Nollau decided he would be happy to know for certain what was likely to happen in the next thousand minutes. For no particular reason other than to occupy an idle corner of his brain, he translated this arbitrary time period into something more practical: it worked out as sixteen hours, twenty minutes. *Now, how far can I expect to get in that time?* he wondered.

He twisted around and looked back: the unidentified island he'd left behind was too far away to make out—or possibly too low on the horizon and swallowed in the night. He returned to a more comfortable seated position and looked ahead. It was difficult to be certain, without a fixed reference point, but he thought he was past the halfway point in his crossing, closer now to the mainland. Once again, he felt his spirits lift. Was he not a proud member of the Master Race? There was nothing he couldn't do if he put his heart and soul into it!

A second later, he shook his head, dismissing this flight of fantasy. He was one man, a long way behind enemy lines in a bitterly fought war that had meandered blindly for year upon year, encompassing most of the globe and still unresolved. He had precious few resources and no money to help him make his way home, and he was further restricted by the mission he had promised to fulfil: to deliver the spear he had salvaged from his stricken vessel to someone who perhaps would understand better than he its significance.

He let his glance fall upon the spear as it came to the forefront of his mind once more, not that it had ever been very far away. The short May night was beginning to fade; the final quarter of the moon had risen and cast a lambent, silvery light on the weapon where he had placed it carefully along the port side of the centreboard. As he gazed at it, it seemed to draw into itself the moonlight, absorbing it before releasing a powerful, pulsating glow as if the natural light had somehow awoken an inner power that had lain dormant for perhaps centuries, since the spear had first been forged in who knew what powerful smith's furnace.

The glow intensified: there could be no doubt about that, but Nollau was not disturbed, or frightened. He sensed that, whatever happened, he was guaranteed as its guardian whatever protection the spear could offer.

He was vaguely aware of the engine note becoming somewhat muted as if it were still running at the same speed but at a distance. His vision blurred, and he felt disorientated, imagining that he and his stolen craft had been plucked from the water by a playful child giant, who had lost interest in this curious toy as quickly as he had found it and tossed it back in the bathtub. What could not be denied, however, was the fact that the engine was now running at normal revs… and reverberating back at him from a set of cliffs which had most definitely still been several miles away before the spear began to glow. A second later, the lightest of crunches beneath the keel confirmed he was in shallow waters. Had he fallen asleep? He thought it unlikely, but there was no other explanation—at least, not a logical one. Still, he wasn't going to refuse the apparent assist with the final stages of his crossing, whatever its source.

The boat rocked gently, and the stern lifted on the swell of a wave, pushing the prow more securely into a gravel bed. Realising he had to get his feet wet anyway, Nollau clambered over the port rail and took a firm grip of the boat. He'd decided he might as well make it look as if it belonged on the shore rather than having been abandoned to float off on the next high tide, which would almost certainly draw unwelcome attention. In a tight-knit Danish fishing community, someone would be bound to know who the boat belonged to; if Nollau wished to avoid immediately raising the alarm, he needed to ensure it also appeared to belong *here*, carefully moored by its rightful owner rather than stolen and abandoned by a marooned submariner.

The prow rested comfortably on the beach, and from the ragged line of seaweed distributed in a gentle arc along the shoreline, Nollau guessed the boat was close to the high-tide point. He fished out the anchor from under the gunwale anyway and dropped it onto the sand, wedging it between two rocks and paying out a generous length of chain to allow it to float if necessary.

As he took the spear back into his arms, his eyes fell on the supply box beneath the seat. There was nothing to keep him there: for the moment, and particularly until he could find some non-military issue clothing, he had to remain either on the move or out of sight during daylight hours, but the temptation to dally and take a hot drink was too much to resist. His tongue curled at the memory of the taste of the acidic, nothing-like-the-real-thing *ersatz* coffee on offer throughout his homeland for the last few years. On the other hand, he'd heard that Danish farmers and fishermen were well-known coffee connoisseurs and could reasonably be expected to have access to supplies of 'the real thing'.

Hardly daring to hope, Nollau reached into the stock cupboard and opened the tin marked 'kaffe'.

Inhaling the rich, chocolaty aroma, Nollau imagined his expression closely resembled that of a cat who has successfully avoided drowning by drinking himself out of Cleopatra's cream bath.

The spirit stove was swiftly assembled, water set to boil, and for the time it took to brew and dispose of three cups of coffee back-to-back, Herbert Nollau was happier than he had been at any time in the last three years. The hit supplied by the rapid consumption of the genuine article after so long enduring the pallid, tasteless substitute on offer in war-torn Germany set his senses dancing with delight. He swilled the fisherman's battered mug with a further splash from the plastic barrel and dried it with a handful of sedge grass. After a few seconds' not-too-strenuous battle with his conscience, he decided to 'liberate' the remaining coffee grounds, carefully moulding the tinfoil package to fit snugly inside the mug, which he hung from his belt. Now he had to weigh his options, none of which appeared particularly attractive.

He could go north or south: to the north was a large town close enough to reach without great difficulty, but he would be travelling in the opposite direction to his ultimate destination, the Fatherland. He couldn't be certain just how many kilometres he had to travel, but it was as near as made no difference the full length of Jylland, the biggest of Denmark's major landmasses, and would take him several days if he had to run and hide all the way. On the other hand, as soon as he could report to a senior officer of the German Occupying Forces, he could hope to fulfil his pledge. The only thing that mattered now was that the spear was returned to the highest echelons of the German command structure. He had to trust that someone, somewhere, had a deeper insight into this mysterious weapon and how it could be used in the *Führer*'s scheme to build a *Reich* that would guarantee Germany's destined role as the unquestioned most powerful nation in Europe, and with that the rest of the world.

South, therefore, was the logical choice. He had no knowledge of how strong his country's hold was in this godforsaken northern pimple on Europe's non-Aryan face, and so his first priority had to be something to help him conceal his true identity and purpose, and preferably a vehicle of some sort. There was many a long league between his current location and his destination, and no chance of concealing his dearly bought prize, the spear, all the way to the German border.

With a rueful glance back at the lights of Frederikshavn, so tantalisingly close, he hefted the spear once more in both hands. This time, Nollau felt a thrill of power flowing from the spear as soon as he touched it—a low hum vibrating from its tip and increasing in volume as it reached the slightly broader butt. The spear glowed with an inner light, and as he turned to face south, there could be no doubt about it: the hum became a purr of approval, encouraging him to begin the long trek.

He began to jog along the beach, keeping to the firm sand that skirted the dunes, curving slightly and always parallel with the water's edge, perhaps fifty metres to his left. Soon, he came to a slipway that led to a wide desire path worn into existence by fishermen's constant use, certainly not permanent enough to deserve being called a road. Still, it had to go somewhere.

The only lighting was the glow from the spear he carried across his body, but it was sufficient for his needs and more useful than the intermittent light from the waning moon, increasingly hidden behind steadily growing banks of cloud. Nollau looked up and frowned: he sensed a change of weather and a near-certainty of rain. Before much longer, he would have to find somewhere to conceal himself for a few hours of rest before the night ended and the world stirred. He had to regard himself as one man against every Dane living in Jylland and assume that anyone he met would do their utmost to prevent him from achieving his goal.

The path meandered slightly uphill, ending at a rough wooden stile: beyond it, a smooth, dark surface suggested a metalled or tarmacked road. Nollau hopped lightly over the stile, full of energy despite his lack of sleep and regular meals. He was more than half convinced that much of this feeling of exceptional health and endurance came from the power he felt every time he grasped the spear. This belief was reinforced by the way it continued to emit a low hum and glowed visibly even before he touched it. He no longer thought of the spear as an inanimate object: there had been too many incidents already to ignore as coincidence, and he was enough of a realist to accept that. There were, after all, many things happening in the world that flew in the face of logic and reason, occurrences that quite simply defied explanation.

The sky was beginning to lighten, yet there were still no signs of habitation nor any structures, isolated or otherwise, where he could rest awhile. As he strode along, he was suddenly aware of a slight but definite pull from the spear, twitching in his grip as if encouraging him to leave the road and cross a field on the left. He hesitated, but only for a second, before he followed the weapon's lead. There was, after all, a limit to how far he could hope to travel on open roads without meeting someone along the way.

There was a somewhat threadbare hedge separating the road from a field—livestock grazing ground, he thought, based on the smell. Not a planted crop, anyway. Following the increasingly impatient insistence of the spear, he brushed through the sparse foliage and stayed low as he crossed the field, heading for a line of trees. Looking left and right, he couldn't see any animals, but daylight had yet to arrive; there could have been a whole herd of cattle standing under the eaves of the woodland he was heading towards, and he wouldn't know it until he was close enough to be trampled to death.

Beyond the treeline, a faint rosy glow signalled the beginning of the day proper, and Nollau paused for a moment. Exactly what day was dawning? He had to think hard about it: each and every day of the past four years or so since he had first entered service in the German Navy had been one of a strict regime, inviolable rules, exact timetables and unvarying patterns of daily routine, all recorded in logs, diaries and other official documents. The first entry on almost every page was, naturally, the date, and often the time, so he wasn't in the habit of having to work out what the day or date might be.

They'd left Lübeck on 3rd May; of that much he was certain, which meant that it was late the following day, 4th May, when his pride and joy *U-534* had met her untimely end. A further day had passed since then, so the new day dawning had to be 6th May—was that possible? So much had happened in such a short period of time! Yet, when he checked once more to make sure his memory wasn't playing tricks on him, he came to the same result.

An overgrown dirt path began at the edge of the woods, and Nollau realised his options were limited. The spear wagged in his hand, encouraging him to trust his instincts and see where the path might lead. Off to his right, he could hear running water and was about to investigate the source when he became aware of a squat structure of some sort to the left of the path.

*Sanctuary!* For some reason, the somewhat archaic term popped into his mind and seemed in the circumstances far more appropriate than 'shelter', though the half-derelict woodsman's bothy was barely that. Nevertheless, the almost-intact roof and sturdy-looking walls seemed unlikely to collapse completely in the few hours Nollau planned to be there, and at that moment, it was as appealing to him as the most palatial hotel room in Berlin. A thick, even mat of grass promised to be as soft as a feather bed for his tired muscles, and there was even a fire grate. As long as the flue above it wasn't obstructed, he could build a fire to warm himself; with a scoop of water from the still-unseen stream, he might even brew another mug of genuine coffee.

*Scheisse!* He'd been lucky once, managing to start a fire by using the glass from his watch, but he had neither the inclination nor stamina to repeat the miracle two days running. Dare he hope that the last occupant had left behind a box of matches?

The hearth and the immediate surroundings were the logical places to investigate first, Nollau supposed. He stood the spear on its butt end, leaning against the rotted doorframe, and started a hopeful fingertip search on the mantel, then along the line of the hearth itself, where the grass was long enough to encroach onto the tiles. A box of matches would be easy to miss. Perhaps *inside* the fireplace itself?

His questing fingertips registered the fact that one brick, the end brick to the right of the fireplace, was not only loose, but it was also scuffed and chipped, far more than its immediate neighbours. Despite the weeds and grass slowly forcing their way through the mortar, this particular brick came away easily in his hand, revealing a small, dry storage compartment containing some small kindling twigs and two—no, three!—boxes of matches. Now, as long as there were still *some* matches in at least *one* of them…

Two of the boxes were part-full, but each held a reasonable number of matches, so means to light a fire, whether for cooking or keeping warm, ought not to be a problem, however long he had to remain a fugitive.

The third box had just two matches in it, but the heads were much bigger and the stems much longer than ordinary matches. They also felt slightly oily. Nollau glanced at the box again but was unable to make sense of the words printed on the back. He surmised the matches were longer lasting than the standard match, and perhaps more difficult to snuff out, but it was by the by. Through the mere act of finding the means to light a fire he felt warmer already, and he went back outside to scavenge kindling.

His mission went momentarily askew when he wandered behind the tumbledown shack and was rewarded by the sight and scent of plump, luscious, perfectly ripe brambles and beyond those, unless he was much mistaken, a similar crop of raspberries. He spent the next fifteen minutes cramming double handfuls of both fruits into his mouth, like a greedy child. Such an extravagance of fresh fruits had long disappeared from the increasingly bare counters of food emporiums throughout Germany. Fresh produce—whether it was meat, vegetables or humble wild fruits such as these—was referred to in whispers below the stairs in some of the few remaining society houses of families who had opted to pull up the drawbridge and sit out the war as best they could in something less than total isolation.

He finally stopped gorging himself when he felt the sugar rush kick in, almost as brutal as the caffeine hit he'd felt back on the strand. Anticipation of a second coffee binge drove him to collect the necessary fuel at a ferocious pace. Soon he was able to leave a healthy fire drawing up the chimney while he scooped a mugful of water from the stream and set it to heat up in the embers. He'd read somewhere that it was more efficient than trying to cook over flames. He'd have to be careful not to blister his fingers when drinking the coffee, and watch for the bitter grounds at the bottom of the mug, but without the luxury of a separate pan, it was his only option.

Shelter, food, heat and the inner warmth of a hot drink: all he now needed was the chance to rest until evening shadows made it possible for him to continue his clandestine journey undetected. Nollau made sure that the fire had died almost to ash: having got this far, he had no wish to attract attention to his presence by burning down the derelict building or to die in a tragic and avoidable accident. He took the spear from the side of the door, laid it with reverential awe in the grass along the back wall of the hovel, curled his body along its length, and was asleep almost as soon as his head nestled on the grass.

# Chapter Thirteen

Flight Lieutenant Roy Burton was accustomed to having his sleep interrupted whenever a scramble was called, but the discreet tap on the shoulder which brought him instantly to full awareness wasn't the usual method of rousing someone who was rostered on-call. He swung his stockinged feet off the bed: other than his boots and tie, he was fully clothed and ready to fly.

"CO's office, Biffo. Solo job, not a full scramble. The CO specifically asked for you and Mick Corcoran for a special op."

"Oh." The single syllable, though delivered neutrally, sounded ominous in the batman's ears. Phil Johnson had been assigned to Roy Burton for the three years he'd been stationed at Minehead—an incredibly long time for any Spitfire pilot to survive daily dogfights against a determined enemy—but Biffo Burton was an exceptionally skilful pilot with an outstanding record of confirmed kills to his name.

Mick joined him as he crossed the gravel parking area outside the CO's office.

"What's the flap, Biffo? Any clues?"

"Not a word, Corky. Phil was sent to pluck me from dreamland and told to do it on the QT."

"Must be a flap of some sort! But just you 'n' me? Has to be a recce, then—it can't be an attack. Nobody in their right mind would send a single Spit up at night for that!"

"Let's beard the lion and find out, shall we?"

*\*\**

Squadron Leader Roger Lyons was perfectly well aware of the full gamut of puns and other word games that had been made of his surname by friend and foe alike throughout his thirty-nine years. He looked up from a document he'd been studying as Roy Burton, senior officer by a whole two days, knocked and entered without waiting for the CO's response.

"At ease, gentlemen. Sit yourselves down. Your mission is vital, and time is short. I asked for you two specifically because of a highly classified flag the top brass have slapped on us, and they believe there may be a direct connection with the jaunt you carried out last Thursday. That being the case, the fewer people who know about this flight, the better."

"And since we're already 'in the know', we're the obvious jockeys for the job."

"Correct, Flight Lieutenant!"

"What's the connection with the bomber escort run over Norway?" Mike Corcoran asked.

"If I read this correctly, it's the secondary mission, the photo survey looking for signs of U-boat activity."

"Really? They must have seen something on the film, then!"

"There's confirmation of that from other sources, but you aren't being sent to the same region. Your target area is due north of the coordinates where you managed to pick up a few vital frames of a hit. There were survivors, I'm told, and they'll be questioned as a priority once they've been treated. We've also got photos from another recce flight, showing more evidence of flotsam from a damaged vessel, so we have to assume that reports of one or more U-boats in the area were correct."

"So, if they were going to meet someone north of there...?"

"Intel thinks the most likely contact would be coming down from a known base well to the north, on Bear Island. A single U-boat, rather than a pack. It's almost exactly a month since von Friedeburg signed the unconditional surrender, but there're still pockets of defiance being mopped up here and there."

\*\*\*

Ten minutes later, Biffo Burton took the controls and taxied to the runway while Corky sat behind him and checked through the assortment of cameras that had been fitted in modified machine-gun emplacements.

*"Point and fire—think of it as squeezing the trigger. It works exactly the same way!"* had been the mechanic's advice, which Mike hadn't asked for.

"I'd be a lot happier if they'd left us with a few more guns!" he groused.

Roy came back to him on the headphones. "Technically, the war's over in Europe, so the chances of us being fired upon are—"

"Don't say it! Don't even think it, Roy! We both know Jerry's not one for playing by the rules, and if there's a sub commander out there still looking to pick a fight, I'd rather know I can defend myself if need be!"

"Point taken, Corky. Let's hope we can get there and back without a problem."

"Fine by me. Are you going to fly this old bucket or fill it with hot air?"

At that moment, Air Traffic Control gave Biffo the green light he'd been waiting for, and they were on their way.

# Chapter Fourteen

HERBERT Nollau woke from a deep, healthy sleep to a full, primal instinct awareness in the space of a single heartbeat. Like a feral cat, he continued to lie completely still, feigning sleep, listening intently. Once he was satisfied that no sudden, untoward sound had roused him, he relaxed, imitating once more the feline habit of stretching muscles which have stiffened during sleep.

A glance at his wristwatch informed him that the time was almost four o'clock, which meant he'd slept almost eight full hours. A second more guilty check confirmed that the clock was still ticking, which was a relief; he'd forgotten to wind it up before crashing into oblivion and had to assume that it was still keeping reasonably accurate time. As if in answer, he heard in the distance four soft chimes as the bells of a village church marked the passing of another hour.

He broke his fast by eating the same diet of high-sugar wild berries he'd had for his supper that same morning and couldn't suppress a wry smile at the thought that the whole day was effectively turned on its head. He remembered vaguely a literary quotation from somewhere about 'going to bed at noon'—could it have been that radical outlaw Shakespeare, banned from all libraries, schools and booksellers in Germany? He rather thought it was. One of the plays, possibly the tragedy, *King Lear*. He shrugged. Right or wrong, the answer wasn't going to help him stay free and on the move.

There was nothing to keep him from leaving, he decided, as he drank from the stream to wash down the last delicious juices of his breakfast. Granted, it was several hours yet before dusk, but he'd seen no-one on the road, and the chances of meeting anyone at all *off* the road had to be considerably longer.

There was no coffee left, so that was one small burden less. Could he be bothered keeping the mug? The answer, of course, had to be 'yes'. He had no idea how long his running and hiding might continue. He once again attached it to his belt and pushed the boxes of matches into his pocket.

Resurrecting the spear from its resting place in the long grass, he carefully wiped its full length with his handkerchief, realising suddenly, in mid-stroke, that he couldn't recall consciously deciding to take out the handkerchief and wondered for one dizzy moment why he was doing this. Was the spear beginning to affect his very thoughts and actions, prompting him to perform acts which he would never have considered if left to his own free will? He shuddered, remembering epic family arguments from his boyhood days between the ultra-right Lutherans and the immovable traditionalist Roman Catholics. The subject of free will had frequently been a bone of contention, resulting in screaming matches and spoilt Sunday dinners. Sometimes he wondered how his parents had ever met, let alone married.

He sloped the spear over his right shoulder and turned slightly in the same direction, stooping to make sure both he and it cleared the sagging doorframe. He didn't really expect a light touch to bring the whole hut tumbling down, but one could never be *too* careful.

Immediately he was outside, and before he could even pose his inner self a conscious thought, he felt the strongest tug yet from the spear. Most unexpectedly, he found he had been whipped around—there really was no other way to describe the sensation—by a real *physical*, if invisible, force.

There could be no doubt about it: the spear was *not* interested in continuing to tramp along the road south he had left, now far out of sight. A steady throb suggested forcefully but not painfully—not yet, at any rate—that his journey continued through whatever lay beyond the stream running at right angles across the far end of the small, unkempt patch of poor grass behind the bothy. But surely that would only lead him *towards* the shoreline, which had to be east rather than the southerly direction he'd decided was the logical way to get back home? He tried to think of a way to check his suspicions, starting by looking for the position of the sun in the sky, wishing he knew the trick of making a shadow on the figures of his wristwatch to find which direction was north. If the sun rose in the east, and appeared to travel clockwise to the west, that meant that during the day it passed in the southern half of the sky.

He stood confused for another few moments, until he was prompted again by an ominously impatient quiver from the spear, which was becoming restless in his hands. *Now you're going too far*, he chided himself. *It may have strange, arcane powers you know nothing about, but it's a piece of wood. Ancient, and no doubt with a fascinating history, but a lump of carbon atoms nonetheless, an inanimate object which positively and categorically can never be a living object imbued with emotions, capable of enforcing its own will on an independent, rational person who happens to have it in his hands!*

All the same, he set off, splashing across the stream almost against his will. Low branches whipped gently at his cheeks, restoring him to a fuller awareness of his surroundings as he floundered through a section of woodland where there didn't seem to be so much as a deer track to follow, nor even a trail made by a smaller animal such as a rabbit. Occasionally, he found himself being guided to the left or the right when the undergrowth between the trees hindered steady progress, but as far as he could tell from feeling the sun on the back of his neck, he was heading back towards the eastern coastline, and it was becoming increasingly difficult for him to exert any control whatsoever over the direction in which he was compelled to move. His breathing became laboured with the exertion until it came in ragged gasps, accompanied by a debilitating stitch just above his hip, which would have amused him were it not such an effort to keep moving. For there could be no doubt about it: inanimate object it might be, but the spear was responsible for what felt like a wide, deathly wound in his side, striking him in exactly the same place as an unnamed Roman centurion was said to have pierced Christ's side on that first long Good Friday, with the Spear of Destiny.

# Chapter Fifteen

"CHRIST, it's cold up here! Are you *sure* the cabin heaters are on, Biffo?"

"Bear Island's not in the Med, you know, Corky. It's actually inside the Arctic Circle, but if you want *real* cold, we could go up a couple of thousand feet instead of wave-hopping to stay below the radar."

"It's OK for you, sitting there with your arse smack on top of the engine. It's right brass-monkey weather back here with the cameras, and I swear the jocks must have missed half the shrapnel holes last time they patched this crate up. It feels like it's blowing half a gale in from somewhere!"

It was nowhere near as bad as Corky was painting it, but Biffo's seat in the tight-packed cockpit was marginally warmer than the relatively less-cramped interior of the Spitfire's fuselage. Without taking his eyes off the screen, Biffo banked slightly to his left to keep a safe distance from another floating ice mountain, then reached down by his right leg as he levelled off.

"If you haven't got a cup, we'll have to share, but as far as I know I'm not carrying anything deadly this week. Got some real coffee last night, down on the docks!"

No self-respecting pilot could resist such an offer—nor would he ever be without a cup of some sort while in the air. Corky had two cups poured and the stopper back on the Thermos before it had a chance to cool.

"How much daylight do we have left?"

"This far north, approaching midsummer? Enough light for decent holiday snaps almost the full twenty-four hours! This is where we should be starting to take shots, though. If there *is* a U-boat trying to meet up with the one we took a pot at—"

"The one we *think* we took a pot at," Corky interrupted before Biffo got carried away.

"All right, I'll grant you we didn't actually get to see it, but Roger as good as said it had been corroborated by another plane, as well as the survivors being picked up."

"Certainly *looks* like a result," Biffo had to admit, "but as I was about to say, we're only guessing where he's coming from, and we don't know whether he's aware there won't be anyone to meet."

"Means we've got a lot of sea to search and one small vessel to find. Oh, Lord, can you say, 'needle, haystack'?"

"We're OK for fuel at the moment, and I can fly her slowly for max. time over the sector while you take pictures. That'll help fuel economy. The boffins say they've tweaked the radar—it's supposed to be more sensitive and more accurate—so that sounds promising as well. Can you run the radar at the same time as the cameras? I'm not keen on using autopilot for very long. I'm concerned about ice forming on the rudder. As far as I can tell, we're clear for the moment, but it's going to get colder."

"Colder than this?"

Corky's elaborate panto gestures weren't entirely an act: the temperature had definitely dropped a degree or two while they'd been drinking their coffee.

"Here's as good a place as any to start the cameras rolling," said Corky, sounding quite chipper despite his complaints about the cold. In truth, he was happiest when taking pictures and had already picked out several promising studios to investigate with a view to starting up as a pro photographer once he'd completed his tour of duty.

Wishing not for the first time that he'd thought to slip on an extra sweater, Corky picked up the headset to the radar and slipped them on, replacing his warm fleece hat over the headband. It was non-regulation, but he found it more comfortable. He had to wait a few moments while the screen turned that distinctly bilious shade of green only ever experienced on radar monitors. Seconds later, he had it off again and was clamouring for Biffo's full attention.

"We need to go about and check that sector again, Sir."

Corky had a habit of remembering rank and manners when he was doing the job he loved. Whether he realised it or not, it made him a popular first dibs when a second man was needed for any sort of special ops in the cramped confines of a Spitfire.

Having noted this, Biffo quietly told himself that he really must find a diplomatic way of pointing out to Corky that volunteering was not the best way to ensure good health and a long life as a fighter pilot. For now, he needed to concentrate on flying through his instruments, as the windscreen was starting to ice over.

"You got anything, Corky? Visual or on the radar?"

"I got a loud *ping* almost before I had the headset on. I'm surprised you didn't hear it yourself!" That wasn't actually possible, but the banter added to the thrill of the chase.

"The water isn't especially deep in this sector, Corky. That's probably why you got a strong reading. She'll be forced to travel close to the surface or risk damaging her hull on the ice."

Biffo climbed and banked westward, chasing the red sliver of sun which squatted awkwardly on the horizon.

"I'll approach from a different direction this time, coming in from the southwest. As long as they don't suss us straight away, a couple of runs and we should be able to nail her to the wall, never mind putting a cross on the map!"

Biffo circled low over the point of North Jylland, skimming over Skagen and thundering out over the Kattegat again, easing back to head due north parallel with the west coast of Norway, more or less mid-channel between the two Nordic countries.

Corky hovered over the camera controls, his hands flying across the buttons of the still-shot cameras. The moving-image cameras were pre-set to run automatically, housed in the nacelle below the cockpit and in the modified bracket which was usually reserved for the tail gunner.

Corky stiffened, then, with an insane grin of triumph, ripped the headphones off and held them six inches from Biffo's ear. Even at that distance, and despite the muted roar of the Merlin engines, the *ping...ping* of radar contact could be heard.

The signal increased in volume and the gap between the blips shortened, indicating they were still approaching. Biffo forced open a side window, letting in a blast of freezing air. The front screen was by now totally opaque and he'd been flying on instruments for the past ten minutes. Glancing out and down, he turned back to Corky and nodded.

"If you can get the window open on your side, you'll see her, no mistaking it! The water's so clear, you can see the lines. I'll throttle back—get as many pics as you can!"

Now dangerously close to stalling speed, Biffo drifted as close to the wavetops as he dared while Corky worked overtime on the manual cameras, keeping half an eye on the smooth running of all the movie cameras. After thirty long seconds defying the laws of gravity, Biffo eased the throttle up a few notches and raised the Spit's nose and allowed the engine to pick up to a higher rate of revs. This time, he opted to climb steeply and circle off to his right, into Norwegian airspace.

"That'll give 'em something to chew on!" he said with a grin as he returned to a few hundred feet above sea level and prepared to make a second pass over the target, heading west by the compass on the dashboard. Once again, the radar bounced off the target, increasing in volume and rapidity of beat as they approached and passed the vessel. It was all over in seconds: Corky marked the map in his hands with a provisional 'X' to tag the coordinates where the flight paths intersected. The information was accurate enough to indicate the U-boat's position to within a nautical mile, provided they hurried back. As long as the skipper had not realised he'd been tagged, it would be child's play to work out how far she might have travelled at any time in the next few hours. Even if the vessel attempted to hide or tack off at a random angle, the choices were limited, and there could only be one outcome.

Biffo was on the radio as soon as he'd finished the second pass and started to climb back to a comfortable height for the dash home.

"Charlie Five to Base. Confirmed sighting, underwater vessel, dimensions within known parameters for Class Seven, repeat, Class Seven U-boat, roughly on the demarcation line of Danish/Norwegian waters, cruising speed only. Last recorded position, mid-channel, southbound and passing Skagen Point, North Jylland. Over."

"Received, Charlie Five. Make for Minehead, use own discretion. No bandits reported in your sector. Over and Out."

\* \* \*

"D'you think he knows he's been spotted, Corky?"

Corky paused in the act of rewinding the film on one of his still-shot cameras.

"Not easy to guess, Biffo. He certainly wasn't in a hurry when we found him, and he seemed to be moving on exactly the same course and at the same rate of knots when we crossed his path the second time, so maybe he was concentrating on navigating the channel. For all I know, their radar might not be tuned to pick up signals from passing planes or even surface vessels if it comes to that. Navigating underwater must be like playing 3D chess blindfolded at the best of times."

"Okay, looks like it's tally-ho for home, slippers and pipe and a nice mug of cocoa!" chortled Biffo, as he opened up the throttle to a full, deep-throated roar and banked slightly left, dropping his nose to generate an extra few mph, hoping to shave a few seconds off their return journey.

\* \* \*

Before Biffo had even taxied to a stop, Corky had slung a bulky satchel containing every exposed reel of film to a waiting motorcyclist, who roared off into the distance while the two exhausted pilots went through their post-flight checks.

"Best show willing, look in and ask if there's anything useful on the film!" muttered Corky.

Biffo looked at him with an odd expression. "You do realise, if we show *too* much interest, we may be lumbered with taking this film and delivering it to whoever needs to study what's on it?"

"No sweat, Biffo. From here, we could be in Inverness or Land's End in less than thirty minutes, and you know it, but we both know where the War Cabinet meets these days, don't we?"

Just in case Biffo missed the point, Corky whistled the opening bars to the folk song 'The Leaving of Liverpool'.

Biffo looked at his watch. "If you think we're likely to be called back for another jaunt, we'd better grab an evening meal while we've the chance!"

"I'd much rather let Associated Press send them down the wires, but the bosses say it's not safe enough for top classified, which these are bound to be."

"So, not only do we get chased off to take these bloody photos, we get to hand-deliver them to Old Winny and the War Cabinet as well! Strewth!!"

"Well, maybe we'll get a cigar each out of it!" Corky riposted as he checked off the final box confirming the Spitfire's airworthiness once fuelled. A fuel bowser drew up alongside the plane as the two pilots climbed down.

\*\*\*

As Corky had predicted, the photos were developed in under an hour, and they were back in the air for the comparatively short hop cross-country to Liverpool. At the side of the runway, waiting for them, was a powerful Norton 350 with sidecar. Waving aside the helmet he was offered by an attendant mechanic, Biffo tightened up the chinstrap of his flying helmet instead. Corky dumped the satchel of film in the sidecar and threw his left leg across the pillion seat.

"There are directions and a map of how to find the War Cabinet buildings..." the mechanic started to say.

Corky looked at him with mild amusement. "Oh, I say! We've got ourselves an Oxford chap trying to tell two Scousers how to find Water Street Station. What a spiffing lark!"

"Shocking, deplorable!" replied Biffo, mock straight-faced. "Don't know what the world's coming to, what, what?"

The young mechanic, who looked barely old enough to shave, turned bright red and turned on his heel, marching off at a high rate of knots.

"You don't think maybe we were a bit harsh on the kid?" asked Corky as he took a moment to follow Biffo's lead and tighten his chinstrap.

"Nah! Anyway, the war's over, at least as far as Europe's concerned. I reckon that lad'll never have to fire a gun in anger." He changed the subject. "Should we just follow the river, then?"

"Speke Boulevard, Aigburth Road, Jericho Lane and The Strand? That's the shortest way I know—unless there's some bomb damage along the way."

"Even if there is, we can go round it on a bike."

"Yeah, you're probably right."

Chipping away at each other and swapping amiable insults, they were out of the airport and heading north, following the flow of the royal-blue Mersey towards the city centre.

\*\*\*

"It's definitely a Class Seven—the latest design we've encountered," was Johnny Walker's comment as soon as he set eyes on the images.

"And from the film shots, he's not exactly in a hurry to get wherever he's going," Peter Yates added. "I mean, let's face it, if you or I were that far from home—and he couldn't be much further from German waters, if he started from Bear Island—we'd surely be trying to make maximum speed all the way. I doubt he's making more than twenty-five knots, and this class of U-boat is capable of almost twice that."

"I'm convinced he intends to rendezvous with someone," Johnny said. "And that would fit with the message from Savage Canary."

He strode back to the wall map of the Kattegat and studied the sparse details they had managed to confirm so far. He tapped on a sector of open sea to the east of a small, triangular island just on the Danish side of a mid-point in the channel separating Denmark from Norway.

"My gut feeling is he's looking to meet someone—we have to assume it's the U-boat we've been chasing—somewhere close to this island." He had to peer closely to read the name printed on the chart. "Damn, it's got one of those funny Danish letters in it. I've no idea how to pronounce it. *Lee-so*? Will that do?"

"It's the only geographical reference point in that sector, unless you go as far south as Anholt," Jim Nolan said. "But that's not what bothers me most. Think about it. Here we've got a powerful U-boat, skulking around and running at half-speed, and the admiral of the German Navy signed the terms of surrender almost a month ago. If he fires so much as a single shot, he's breaking the terms of that treaty, and committing a deliberate act of war."

"If he doesn't intend to fight all the way home, why is he dawdling?" Jim demanded. "Why isn't he going like the clappers? And what possible purpose is served by stopping to meet up with another U-boat?"

"There must be either a person or an item of cargo, which for some reason has to be transferred from the one to the other," Jim suggested. "And unless the one we've been tracking is going to turn around and accompany this one back to Germany, my hunch is that the transfer will be from the southbound vessel to the rogue heading *away* from home base. It would be so much easier to understand if we had a clue why he's heading away from home waters, particularly so long after the declaration of surrender was signed. I still haven't worked that one out!"

"There has to be a reason for the U-boat we've been tracking making the trip in the first place," Johnny Walker said. "I'm inclined to believe that the purpose of the journey has to be to smuggle whatever it is *away* from Germany."

"There's just one problem," Peter Yates said "We can't get any of our vessels to the area in time to prevent the meeting—nor witness it, more's the pity. The only way we'll see anything is by scrambling a couple of Spits, with strict orders not to fire so much as a single shot."

"Well, it'll have to be someone else, this time!" Biffo said, secure in the knowledge that they were too far from the relevant sector of the North Sea to be pressed into service for a third sortie within twenty-four hours.

"Amen to that, and cheers!" Corky added, raising a coffee mug of impressive proportions to emphasise his point.

"All the same, you can earn your keep while you're with us," Peter Yates insisted, "because the thoughts of a pilot who's still on active duty would be *very* useful. We've so little hard evidence to go on, we're dancing in the dark at the moment."

Biffo was immediately interested. He'd been studying the charts and had managed to work out for himself—so he thought—what most of the signs, symbols and handwritten notes meant. "What d'you need to know?"

"Well, the speed of the U-boat is, frankly, mystifying," Johnny Walker said. "It's neither one thing nor the other!"

Briefly, he told the two pilots the facts the War Council team had established regarding the actual speed of the target vessel, compared with the speeds it was capable of achieving and which would normally have been expected of a ship of any sort attempting to run for home through potentially hostile waters. "For a while, we thought it might be one last act of defiance, an attempt to hinder the planned homecoming of Prince Haakon of Norway, but if they continue at their present speed and on the current course, they're not going to be anywhere remotely close to where the crossing will take place."

As if the point needed reinforcing, he tapped a pointer on the harbour at Frederikshavn.

Jim Nolan looked at the wall clock, which showed a few minutes past midnight. "If everything went to schedule, gentlemen, I can inform you that the Crown Prince should have arrived home yesterday, in which case, we can be certain that our target is not intending to cause any sort of diplomatic incident of that nature. Which leaves us with our original theory that they intend to meet the other U-boat and transfer cargo unknown."

"Assuming our received intelligence was accurate and we haven't been chasing a ghost for the last four days and more!" growled Jim Nolan, who was beginning to have serious doubts about the whole business.

Johnny Walker rounded on this immediately. "I remind you, we found considerable evidence of an underwater explosion, and we've a full complement of about fifty crew as PoWs on Anholt."

Jim nodded his apologies. "Sorry, Johnny, it's getting late, and I'm not thinking straight, but you're right, of course. Next point?"

"Does this alleged second U-boat know that the vessel they're trying to meet has been sunk? That the meeting can't take place?"

"We can only guess, but if it were *my* command, I'd be in constant radio contact with the other vessel, and I'd be extremely concerned if I wasn't getting a response to my signals. We have to assume he's aware that there's a problem."

"Likely response, Johnny? This is *your* special field, I think?"

Johnny thought for a while.

"Given the circumstances—and if he knows about the same as *we* do and can guess a bit more from whatever contacts he may have had with the other vessel and the German High Command—he hasn't got much of a choice. From his last known position, he's entering Danish coastal waters. By now, he *must* have heard that the cessation of hostilities documents have been signed, in which case he'll be under orders not to fire at any Allied Forces ships or anything else he encounters en route for his home base."

"Yes, I'd buy that one," Peter agreed. "So, what next?"

"In his position," said Johnny, "there's only one thing he could do."

# Chapter Sixteen

Nollau was close to stumbling at every other step as he followed the urgent throb pulsating the length of the spear, snaking up his arm and across his shoulders. He felt a glow spread across his chest, easing his laboured breathing, giving his heart a shot of something which made the hundred-plus beats a minute seem like a sedate sixty. Boundless energy coursed through his lower body, too: the muscles in his thighs pumped more readily, his feet moving unerringly from one secure spot to another without him needing to concentrate on avoiding unseen obstacles. He felt more alive than he had ever felt before and acknowledged to himself that the sudden influx of surplus energy had an external source, one over which he had no control.

He could no longer feel the ground beneath his feet. Was he flying, floating, hovering above the undergrowth and bushes which grew so tight between the tree boles? He couldn't resist the urge to glance down as he leapt from one point to another—no, he was certain that his foot had definitely touched that bush before he took another elongated slow-motion stride through the forest, each ground-eating pace in excess of two metres.

Even if he'd wanted to, which he didn't, there was no question of him releasing his grip on the spear. It was almost as if his palm had become fused to the smooth wooden shaft, yet this didn't concern him. He could feel the power flowing throughout his body, emanating from the ancient weapon he carried, and it seemed no longer frightening or unnatural but the most normal thing in the world.

Without warning, he reached the last fringe of trees, which stopped dead at a line of rocks. Beyond the rocks, any ambitious roots from the forest would have had great difficulty establishing themselves or obtaining sustenance from the sandy beach that ran down to the waters of the Kattegat. He glanced to his left and made out the shape of an island in the mid-distance: juggling times and distances in his head, he was almost certain it was the island he had sailed away from the previous day. The spear was suddenly quiescent in his hands, and he had a brief, lucid moment for coherent thought. After all the ingenuity he had shown following the sinking of his command ship, and the sheer physical effort he had put into his attempt to flee south, was he really being forced to return to the sector of the North Sea where everything had started to go wrong? The spear hummed once more in his hand, a pleasant, melodic major chord as if it had heard the unspoken question forming in his mind.

Next he knew, he was sitting on a convenient flat rock without any memory of making a conscious decision to do so. He watched his fingers untie his bootlaces, feeling detached from the whole process, as if it were someone else performing this mundane task. He placed the boots to one side, his socks balled together, tucked inside. His trousers he rolled up neatly to just below his knees. Picking up the spear once more, he straightened his back and marched with the weapon over his right shoulder until he reached the gentle wavelets lapping at the edge of the beach.

He waded out until the water reached his thighs and his toes began to sink into a soft sand-and-mud mixture. Without hesitating, he reached out and clasped the spear with interlocked fingers just below the forged metal tip.

He laid his body along the shaft: it felt comfortable, natural, right.

He began to paddle with his arms, knowing as he did so that he was in no danger of losing his balanced or falling off, despite the narrow gauge of the spear's shaft. It had become so much an extension of his arms, and through his arms, the rest of his body, that he simply *knew* it would not betray him in such a fashion, especially not now.

It seemed all that was required of him was to make the effort to launch the spear from the shallowest water close to the shoreline. He had put in perhaps twenty or thirty overarm strokes before he felt the tug of the spear once more. This time, it was more subtle, less demanding: he thought this a sign that he had understood the weapon's intentions. Could an object such as this possibly have such things as intentions? The shaft took on the now-familiar internal luminescence he had seen come and go at various stages of the journey and aimed itself at the newly risen sun to the east. Though the North Sea waters were cold all year round, even now in midsummer, the spear itself radiated warmth, and Nollau was grateful.

The power the spear was generating increased gradually until the speed of passage raised a small bow wave, which caused Nollau some discomfort, splashing into his nostrils and mouth, making it difficult to breathe. The logical thing to do, he decided, was to stand, giving himself some distance from the curling, rushing water which was threatening to choke him.

Somehow, he knew exactly where to place his bare feet on the shaft, to achieve a comfortable, balanced position just aft of the centre point. Extending his arms, right shoulder slightly ahead of his left and a fraction higher, he leant into the wind, which pummelled at his cheeks as his speed increased still further. The butt end of the spear dug a fraction deeper into the waves as he automatically altered his weight distribution, and the rumble of his passage keened up to a powerful *hiss!* as the friction of the wooden shaft carving through the water faded and his speed increased yet again. He had no idea where this voyage might end, but he was unafraid. The spear was now in full control of that: all Nollau had to do was give himself over to the exhilaration of this undreamed-of method of transport.

The repetitive bounce of shaft on wave became negligible, and even with his eyes closed, he knew his speed had increased still further. Contact with the water became minimal, and the rush of wind was suddenly the only noise he could hear. Looking down, beneath his feet, he saw that he was now flying in long hops measuring perhaps a hundred metres at a time, maybe more. Without a fixed point of reference, it was impossible to judge how much time was spent in the air between each caress of the wave tips, but he was certain that the gaps between landings were becoming longer every time, and he realised that soon—very soon—he might become the first person in recorded history to achieve unassisted flight.

\*\*\*

Two Spitfires from RAF Minehead patrolled Kattegat at opposite ends of a large, oval course from a position just south of the island of Anholt to a northern marker above the Norwegian capital, Oslo. They held a watching brief only, though in private, both pilots felt almost naked without the reassurance of knowing they were fully armed and in a position to defend themselves against hostile fire. It was all very well for the squadron leader to refer time and time again to the 'end of hostilities' document which had been signed, but *he* wasn't the one with his arse on the seat, flying a crate loaded with cameras and film instead of bullets and rockets.

In their briefing, they'd been told what to look for: one of the latest Class VII U-boats trying to sneak south unobserved, rather than running at full power through enemy waters.

"The water's not particularly deep, at least as far as a U-boat's concerned. We think there's a very good chance he'll surface somewhere off the Danish coast and attempt a rendezvous with another vessel—almost certainly another U-boat," the squadron leader had explained. "You must at all times remember that the end of the war in Europe officially dates from the day the treaty was signed. I grant you that was only four days ago, and it's possible that some of the more far-flung military and naval units have either not heard the official announcements or are continuing to put up a fight despite orders to the contrary."

"So, you're asking for decent, detailed photographs, which means us getting in low enough for Jerry to use us for target practice, anyway, even if some admiral's scribbled his name on a piece of paper thousands of miles away?"

"It's only a couple of hundred miles to the nearest German border from there, but that's not the point. We cannot be seen to do *anything* which could be construed as an open act of war during these first few fragile days of peace. Is that understood?"

It was understood, but not popular. The begrudged, "Yes, Sir," from both pilots was clear evidence of their feelings, but none of that mattered now, as they circled and circled over the sector of Kattegat where the bandit was expected to surface.

"Hope these coordinates are right, Charlie!"

They were now on their third sweep over the Kattegat, covering a sector of the North Sea between Oslo in the north and a small island named Anholt roughly at a midpoint between Denmark and Sweden, their landmark for a return back north. Without looking up from the spectrum of viewfinders and camera lenses he was concentrating on, the navigator shrugged.

"If we *do* see a bogey, you'd better hope they've had orders not to open fire. I feel naked without so much as a pea-shooter on board!"

"Wait a minute! There's something there. Hang on! I'm going in for a closer look!"

With the lightest of touches, Ed Holmes banked the Spitfire steeply left and put his nose down to swoop from a cruising height of two thousand feet to level at barely two hundred. Throttling back to as slow a speed as he dared without risking a stall, he returned to the target area from the west. The waters here were clear and relatively shallow: there was nowhere a vessel of any size could hope to run and hide.

"Foxtrot Alpha to Chicken House."

"Roger, Foxtrot Alpha, go ahead."

"Surface activity, we have contact. Repeat, we have contact. Single bogey surfacing, no sign of any further vessels in this sector. Radar is clear."

A brief pause followed, during which Ed caught Charlie's eye in the cockpit mirror. Charlie nodded and accompanied his nod with a thumbs up.

"Chicken House, I can confirm the bogey is a U-boat, identified as a Class Seven. Position is about five clicks east of a small island in mid-channel, southeast of Frederikshavn. Charlie, read off the name of the island while I go around again."

Charlie read off L-a-e-s-o, using the phonetic alphabet to get around the unfamiliar Scandinavian letters æ and ø. Both pilot and navigator were extremely conscious of the fact that they had no defences whatsoever, should the skipper of the U-boat decide to take a pot at them, either in defiance of the newly signed terms of surrender or because he genuinely had not had notification that the war was over.

"It's all very well for Winny and the boys in the backroom to say 'We will not be the first to blink or break our solemnly given word about observing a total ceasefire', but it's not them with their arse in a sling, sitting in a manky stitched-up, patched-together Spit which hasn't had a proper service in over six months!" Ed turned once more. This time, he banked to his right, over Sjælland to approach the target sector from the south, get an alternative point of view for Charlie's cameras.

Twice the RAF's eyes and ears circled the plotted course, capturing every detail of the Class VII U-boat, glistening as if newly delivered from a pristine assembly line in the most up-to-date factory in Europe. Despite its undoubted purpose as a fearsome weapon and its proven ability to deliver death and destruction, there was a certain savage beauty to the vessel. The morning sunlight caught the last of the seawater cascading from the fuselage back into the sea, as if absolving her from the guilt of all her sins.

"Foxtrot Alpha to Chicken House. Activity on deck, logged at 0915 Zulu. Coordinates are as follows…"

Charlie passed Ed a note with a six-figure map reference, which Ed read back to base.

"Foxtrot Alpha, investigate on your next pass."

"Copy that, Base. ETA over target nest time, 0930 Zulu."

\* \* \*

Five minutes before this activity, beneath the calm waters of Kattegat, the skipper of *U-3503* had taken the final decision he would make as commander of the vessel.

"Attention all hands. Don life jackets. Prepare to abandon ship. Report to your assigned lifeboat stations."

It went against the grain for him to give the order, and he had purposely driven himself, his crew and his vessel more than halfway home from Bear Island before revealing the orders of the day he had received in a private coded message just after leaving the base. He had hoped to be able to reach German waters before being forced to surrender, but he was realistic enough to admit that his chances were minimal.

He continued issuing the instructions as they appeared in his last signal.

"Do not take personal equipment off the vessel. Do not carry any item or document which could be a security issue or which might be considered a weapon of any sort. When you are questioned, remember that the Geneva Convention only requires you to give your name, rank and number. Ensure that you are not carrying anything which would reveal any other facts or details of your background, your family, your duties and responsibilities as a member of this crew."

\*\*\*

"Foxtrot Alpha to Chicken House. Bogey confirmed at 0926 Zulu. ID markings on conning tower read *U-3503*. She appears to be holding a static position. The crew are leaving in lifeboats, in an orderly fashion. There are no signs of damage—a white flag is being tied to the superstructure, Chicken House. It would appear that the commander of the vessel is surrendering. I repeat, white flag is being flown, *U-3503* appears to be surrendering. Over!"

There was a brief pause, then a new voice spoke in Ed's earpiece.

"Foxtrot Alpha, this is Squadron Leader Peter Yates of the Joint Armed Services. You are to overfly the lifeboats and guide them in the direction of the nearest landfall, which is a small island called Læsø approximately three miles east of your current location. Act as shepherd to the flock and make sure they comply, but do not use force or intimidatory tactics."

"Roger, Chi–Sir! There is no radar activity on my screen," he continued, glancing at his instruments, "and if it was the commander's intention to meet up with another vessel, it would seem the other vessel has been prevented from making the rendezvous."

"Acknowledged, Foxtrot Alpha. Your brief is to keep watch over the scene until another plane can be dispatched to relieve you. How's your fuel situation? Over."

"Roger, Chicken House. We still have more than half tanks of fuel—estimate we can remain on station for another three hours, but we'd be pushed to get home by then. Over."

"Understood, Foxtrot Alpha. Expect relief plane before eleven hundred Zulu."

\* \* \*

The sun rose, blood red and dripping wet, from the unbroken line of watery horizon directly ahead. Nollau stood tall on the spear, somehow seeming to have gained in stature as he rode easily on the impossibly narrow baseboard. He might have been the blueprint for the blonde Aryan warrior figure which his defeated leader's attempts at genetic engineering had failed to produce.

All his tiredness was now forgotten; all his physical discomforts had disappeared. Whether he realised it or not, he was now riding the perfect wave that a generation still unborn would spend the whole of their lives searching for, without success. Onward he sped, unafraid, spending less and less time in kiss-contact with the gently lapping wave tips, longer hanging in the clear air between leaps and touchdowns.

\* \* \*

"Chicken House, this is Foxtrot Alpha. Have just observed a green signal from *U-3503*, over."

"Acknowledged, Foxtrot Alpha. Stand By."

A short pause.

"Foxtrot Alpha, we are receiving a 'clear' message on International Distress Frequency five hundred kilohertz. Message is in English and reads as follows.

"From Commanding Officer *U-3503*, Kattegat, Danish sector. Acting on instructions from German High Command, I confirm total and immediate surrender of this vessel in accordance with the Cessation of Hostilities document signed on 4th May 1945 by Admiral Karl Dönitz and others, in the presence of Field Marshal Montgomery. I claim all the rights and protection as defined in the Geneva Convention for my crew, which is currently leaving the vessel on my orders. For myself, I reserve the right to choose to go down with my ship. Heil Hitler!

"Message ends. There is no signature to identify the commander."

"Foxtrot Alpha, this is your relief crew in Delta Bravo, breaker, breaker!"

The unexpected link message from another plane set the pulses of all the listeners racing, and the pilot's choice of the shortcut code 'breaker' indicated urgent new information.

"Delta Bravo, go ahead." As pilot at the sharp end, Ed Holmes took automatic responsibility to respond, rather than wait for his superior officer in the War Cabinet to pull rank on him.

"Apologies, Chicken House, we have an update on your situation, Foxtrot Alpha. There is a small vessel, possibly not a vessel, it's travelling so fast it could even be a rocket or missile of some sort! It's approaching your coordinates at a high rate of knots. Intermittent wake suggests it is flying close to sea level, with occasional touchdown splashes.

Appears to be locked on to the coordinates given for U-3503."

\* \* \*

Back in the underground bunker in Liverpool's Water Street, Johnny Walker stiffened. "Remember the Dambusters?"

Nods all round. Nobody needed reminding of the spectacular success of May 1943, when 617 Squadron had destroyed a supposedly impregnable German dam using a bouncing bomb invented by Barnes Wallis.

"Delta Bravo, close in and get any photos you can. Identify if possible, whether vessel, plane, rocket..."

"Ten-Four, Chicken House. Time's tight, but I'll give it a go. Tally-ho!"

The radio went abruptly dead as Delta Bravo suited action to word.

\* \* \*

Herbert Nollau was on a natural high. He'd never considered experimenting with drugs, had never even tried tobacco and drank very little, even on formal social occasions. He had nothing from personal experience with which he could compare his present euphoric state of sheer bliss and wanton abandon. He felt a scream of victory welling from somewhere deep inside, starting from his diaphragm, pushing every last scrap of air from his over-inflated lungs, emerging at last from the constraints of a throat too tight to contain the ululation. A wordless howl burst from his lips which at the last possible second became a single word, magnified beyond the power of any normal human voice:

"*VALHALLAAAAAAAAAAAAAAAAA!!*"

The spear rose majestically from the wave tips one final time, accelerating to a blur of white-hot light, impaling

*U-3503* through and through at the base of the conning tower. Cut clean in half, its back broken, the nose and tail pirouetted vertically for an impossible second, then two, before sinking gracefully out of sight, eerily soundless.

As the two halves of the stricken sea wolf disappeared from sight, the water roiled and boiled, ripping outwards, pushing at the stragglers amongst the submariners in their lifeboats as if to shoo a flock of innocent ducklings away from the danger of an unseen pike or other predator intent on making them its next meal.

The pilot of the relief plane, Delta Bravo, could only watch with a mixture of horror and awe as the scene unfolded. As he said in his first verbatim report on landing...

"Watching what happened, I somehow *knew* the lifeboats were in no danger, and yes, in an odd way, I think I *do* believe that the first pressure wave was meant to carry the last of the lifeboats out of the danger zone before the final blast..."

...which everyone was expecting, knowing it was inevitable. When it did at last arrive, it began as a deep rumble felt by many on the shores of Læsø. Others reported feeling 'something' at various points along the coast, from Grenå in the south, as far north as Frederikshavn, and even in Skagen.

At least two full minutes ticked and winked out of existence before a waterspout began to grow rapidly—and, eerily, in total silence—from the point at which the twin halves of *U-3505* had disappeared. Vixen One continued to film. At its highest, the column of water grew to just over two hundred metres before it began to subsume and collapse. As well as the general detritus and flotsam of ruined equipment, machine parts and twisted, wrecked pieces of fuselage, there was also the odd pathetic reminder of the human lives miraculously spared which *could* have been lost: a few personal possessions, such as socks, trousers, a radio, a shoe.

In the weeks to come, when all the evidence it had been possible to salvage had been ferried in, catalogued, examined and labelled, there would also be an unlooked-for bonus for scientists and marine biologists, who would discover no less than thirteen new additions to the planet's known flora and five hitherto unknown forms of marine animal life, lifted from the seabed by the force of the underwater explosion.

\*\*\*

Jim Nolan didn't like discrepancies, and there was something he still couldn't rightly pinpoint in all the evidence from the last moments of *U-3503*.

"This explosion," he grunted as he shared a lunchtime beer with Peter Yates in the Ship & Mitre. "It shouldn't have been possible, not if the captain was telling the truth about not carrying explosives. I've got the feeling it's staring me in the face, but there must be *something* we haven't factored into the equation."

"Did you ever decide what it was Delta Bravo reported heading towards the scene at a high rate of knots? He wasn't sure if it was a surface vessel, a light plane, even a missile of some sort?"

"That's the curious thing." Jim flipped a stack of still photos at Peter. "Here, in the last few seconds of film, it looks to me for all the world like a lance or a jousting pole—no, that's not right. A spear perhaps? And that looks like a man—a figure of some sort, anyway—standing on it, riding it."

"I see what you mean, Jim," Peter said, pushing the photos back to his associate. "But that's not going to cause an explosion, either...is it?"

# About the Author

Born in the Year of the Tiger, Paul has always had the feline instinct to roam.

After spending most of his teaching career as an eternal supply teacher throughout Europe, Liverpool's siren song was too strong to resist, so Paul came home and got himself a 'proper job' writing books.

Just one dream still unfilled: to buy a horse and caravan and hide on the country lanes of Roscommon.

To find out more about Paul's books, visit
www.paulmcdermottbooks.com

# Also by Paul McDermott

*Taking the Heat*

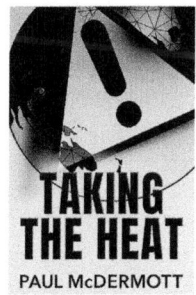

Everybody talks about the weather...
...but nobody does anything about it.

Right?
Wrong!

Human action (or inaction) has forced the delicate balance of the Earth's health close to an irreversible tipping point.

Under the remote command of the elusive Brigadier Groth, Doctor Joey Hart and his maverick team get **one shot** at solving the problem.

*If they dare...*

beatentrackpublishing.com/PaulMcDermott

# Beaten Track Publishing

For more titles from Beaten Track Publishing, please visit our website:

https://www.beatentrackpublishing.com

Thanks for reading!

Printed in Dunstable, United Kingdom

64312092R00099